Ruthless Pantheons: Act 1

Disclaimer:

This book is a work of fiction inspired by various mythologies, religions, and pantheons. The characters, events, and settings are entirely imaginative and not meant to represent or disrespect any deity, religious figure, or belief system.

Elements from different traditions have been creatively reinterpreted to build a unique fantasy world. These adaptations are for storytelling purposes and should not be seen as accurate depictions of real-world beliefs.

This book explores themes of power, conflict, and growth through a fantastical lens. It is not intended to critique or diminish any religious or cultural beliefs. Additionally, it contains sensitive topics that may not be suitable for all readers.

Any resemblance to real people, places, or events is purely coincidental.

Thank you for your understanding and for embarking on this journey.

Prologue: The only true wisdom is in knowing you know nothing." , Socrates

The purpose of life. Humanity's greatest curiosity. Every human at one point thought of it. Some turned to religion, others to philosophy. But what if. What if the answer is something beyond our control?

"So the 532nd cohort has been selected" someone said, every syllable palpating with power.

"Why do you sound so bored?" chirped another, this one more cheerful. A hint of playfulness and mischief in his eyes.

"Enough, I will gain a champion to put yours to shame." another voice declared. Daring and menacing.

"I suppose there is always a chance that this cycle will present greater entertainment." the original voice stated. As if to console the other two.

Then they all turned to a screen, passing coins to each other. I wonder what it is they are watching. Will we ever know?

Chapter 1: "Appearances are often deceiving" , Aesop

Getting terrified by a child wasn't exactly on my agenda today. Hi, I'm Hudson Mitchell. Most people would probably describe me as "troubled." Growing up, I always knew I was different from other kids; I never seemed to fit in. I felt like an outsider looking in. The reason was unbeknownst to me. Needless to say, this made life complicated.

Early on I was labelled as "different". What nobody tells you is that people don't like "different." Adults pretend to be polite, masking their discomfort behind a facade. But children? They don't even have the ability to hide it. They haven't learned social norms yet; they speak their minds, without empathy, without fear of consequences. There wasn't a day I didn't return to my place of rest as the target of some new prank. And when I returned to what was supposed to be "home," my foster parents would scold me for the mess I'd made, as if enduring the abuse was my fault.

But I survived. I worked hard, determined to get the grades needed for university. And here I was studying history, the one subject that actually interested me. However, I didn't know what to expect; I had never known the meaning of freedom. Some of you reading this might understand how I felt. I wasn't excited, nor was I expecting any sort of catharsis. Truth be told, I was anxious. And the last thing I expected at university was what I ended up with: boredom.

To play devil's advocate, I never really socialised. What was the point? Why share my story? Nothing ever changes, people don't change. It felt as if my presence alone was enough to irritate others. I could see how people reacted to me before I even had a chance to speak.

Life was monotonous. The lectures came and went, assignments piled up, but I could never shake the feeling that I didn't belong here. While others joined societies, made friends, and partied the nights away, I retreated further into my shell. I had survived years of foster care, bullying, and a society that didn't want me. University was just another battleground, and I was a soldier who had seen too many fights to care about winning this one.

Then came the day everything changed.

[Criteria Has Been Met]
[Synchronisation 100%]
[Now Preparing Tutorial]
May the Ancient Deities of all Realms Guide You.

Two distinct voices suddenly invaded my mind, one monotonous and almost mechanical, the other more human, yet oddly irritating despite its well-meaning tone. Before I could even process what they were saying, exhaustion hit me like a freight train. My body felt heavy, and with the unnatural weight on my eyelids, it was only a matter of time before I collapsed.

When I woke up, I found myself in an unnaturally bright, white room. It took me a few seconds to gather my bearings, but when I did, I realised I wasn't alone. There were four others besides me. A slightly overweight man was frantically demanding answers from no one in particular. Two women, identical in appearance but starkly different in demeanour, one with a hawk-like gaze that hinted at hostility, the other clinging to her twin's shoulder, head buried. And then there was a child, no older than twelve. She didn't seem out of place because of her age, but rather due to the look in her eyes. A look I recognized all too well. The look of superiority.

"Congratulations, mortals," she spoke with a detached air, her voice uncannily similar to the one I had heard earlier. "You've all been granted the honour of entering the endless realms."

I had more questions than answers, and I wasn't alone. "What the hell do you mean, 'mortals'? Who are you, why did you bring us here?" The man wasn't a complete fool; despite his outburst, he asked the right questions, just at the wrong time.

"Shawn Alexander Adams… Do not interrupt me" the oracle stated, venom dripping from her voice. Her eyes momentarily reflect the power of the sun.

That shut Shawn up, and terrified the rest of us, because at that moment, we all realised the true power hidden behind the shell of this innocent-looking child.

"Now, before I was so rudely interrupted, I was about to explain why you're here and introduce myself. Rejoice, this is your opportunity to exceed your potential and become more than your mortal seal. The council of gods seek power and bestow on you the privilege of gaining their blessings. As for who I am, I have been known as both Pytho and Pythia, but you shall address me with respect. You'll come to know me best as the Oracle of Delphi."

As she stood there, a malevolent grin stretching across her face, I couldn't help but recall the words I'd heard before being brought here: *May the ancient deities of all realms guide you.*

The air in the room thickened as the weight of her words settled in. The child, or rather, the Oracle, was not some fantasy or hallucination. We had been transported, whether physically or mentally, into a space that defied all logic I had ever known.

Shawn remained quiet now, his earlier bravado replaced with uncertainty. The twins, too, seemed rattled, though the more dominant of the two was doing her best to mask it. And the Oracle? She looked like she was enjoying our confusion.

"You four have been chosen to represent humanity in the trials of the Endless Realms. Succeed, and you will achieve dreams beyond your greatest desires. Fail..., let's just say that failing isn't an option."

My heart pounded in my chest. This was some kind of sick joke, right? Trials? Endless Realms? It sounded like something straight out of a dystopian novel. Yet, the gravity in the Oracle's voice left little room for doubt. Whatever was happening, it was very real. Yet the fear that I expected myself to find was nowhere to be seen, instead excitement took its place.

Chapter 2. "Fate leads the willing, and drags along the reluctant." , Seneca

Out of the corner of my eye, I noticed the twins whispering to each other, as if devising a battle plan. Then, the more timid of the two mustered the courage to speak up, seeking clarity, "Oh great Oracle of Delphi, Servant to Apollo, why were we chosen, and what is our task?"

That's where I heard the name before. *The Oracle of Delphi*, the seer of prophecy, servant to the Greek god Apollo. That is who she was.

The Greek seer smirked in response. "It's refreshing to see some respect. To answer your question, you've all been brought here for an opportunity. An opportunity for greatness. An opportunity to become the very gods you mortals once worshipped in your history."

I didn't buy it, something was off. I was skeptical, and thankfully I wasn't the only one who felt that way. One of the twins was looking at the oracle with distrust plastered on her face. The other twin's expression was blank, perhaps it was due to shellshock, perhaps something else entirely, who am I to say. But unfortunately, one of us looked at the seer through rose tinted lenses.

"So with the help of pagan gods can I achieve power? Can I really become a god?" exclaimed Shawn, now looking at the oracle with awe.

The oracle paused for a moment, her eyes glancing over Shawn, before she decided to ignore him completely. "Instead of explaining everything to you, it's easier for you to experience it yourself." She snapped her fingers, summoning a card to each of our hands with writing on them.

A moment of silence passed, and then shock spread across everyone's faces. Despite the tension, I couldn't help but smile, knowing my mundane world was about to become extraordinary

Name: Hudson Mitchell
Rank: Mortal (F)
Class: N/A
Patrons: N/A

Skills:
- **Identify**
- **Low Pain Resistance**
-

"As I am certain you have all noticed," she continued. "This world is no longer what you once knew. You are now capable of greater things. You will obtain patron deities, the council of deities decided to give you the aid of the system after the 400th cycle, you should consider yourself lucky. You at the very least have the capacity of knowing yourselves using the cards that you have been gifted" Her words carried a heavy weight.

"The cohorts before you, through the grace of the gods, gained permission to aid you in your trials. The class system was created using the gods' mercy." It felt to me that there was more for her to mention. But how am I meant to know the mindset of an oracle? Nevertheless, I had to ask what I needed to know.I glanced around at the others; skepticism was written all over their faces, brows furrowed and lips tight. Meanwhile, Shawn looked back at us, nodding slowly with a vacant expression, clearly just as lost, but for entirely different reasons.

"Miss Oracle, will our classes be unique to us?" I asked, trying to be respectful.

Her eyes glanced over me similarly to how they glanced over shawn, with a trace of a golden glow. "Hudson, the class you're about to choose will be basic, but it can evolve in very specific ways. Be sure to choose wisely." she concluded without caring to elaborate,

After that remark, the twin with fury in her eyes began to speak. "Okay so why are we here with them?" the oracle looked at the girl waiting for more. "-Miss oracle" the girl finally added.

The oracle was slowly losing her patience, "you will understand your place soon. Choose your class and weapon." Then with a wave of her hand we were transported to individual rooms.

The oracle appeared before me with a wide grin.

I stared at the table before me, wondering what would happen next. The answer came before my eyes.

It is now time to choose a class.
Analysing mortals.
3 potential matches found.

Assassin.
A master of stealth, precision, and speed. This class excels at eliminating enemies quickly and efficiently. Assassins are lightly armoured, relying on agility as opposed to brute strength or heavy defences. You will need to have cunning tactics and an eye for the shameless.

To think I'm a natural assassin, who would've thought? But despite the allure of this class and the power behind the names of its I knew that running from confrontation wasn't my style.

Heavy Warrior.

Tenacious, tanky and terrifying . Clad in the sturdiest armour and wielding massive weapons, this class is built to withstand tremendous damage while dealing powerful, crushing blows. Use brute strength to control the battlefield and protect allies. This class is ideal for mortals who prefer a tanky, defensive playstyle. You will be a centerpiece to the battlefield, unstoppable, unbreakable, unmoveable.

Now this was more like it, no running from combat, just pure strength and resilience. But I couldn't shake the feeling that there was something even more fitting for me. My instincts, which I always trust, told me there was still more to explore.

Light Warrior.
Powerful, fast, yet subtle. What lies between all other classes, the most versatile with the most room to grow. You will need to have adaptive instincts for you will never be in simply one role. You will need tactical acumen, and a natural instinct for victory.

This was it. I instantly knew this was the class I wanted, rather, the class I needed. I couldn't explain why, it just felt right. Without any further hesitation, I made my decision.

Beep!
You have chosen [Light Warrior] as your first class.
Your presence has expanded
May the ancient deities of all realms guide you.

Chapter 3. "Set your life on fire. Seek those who fan your flames." , Rumi

After I chose my class, the oracle gazed at me with a slight, knowing smile. "Now," she began in her calm, measured voice, "you have ten minutes to ask any questions before the tutorial begins. Use your time wisely."

The atmosphere felt heavy, filled with both anticipation and the weight of the choices I had just made. Finally, the ball was in my court. I had the chance to ask what I truly wanted to know, and I intended to make the most of it.

I thought for a moment before speaking. "Miss Oracle, when I selected my class, I was promised a weapon to assist me, but I have yet to receive it. How do I go about obtaining this aid?" I thought it was a practical question to start with, given how crucial a weapon would be in the trials to come.

The oracle sighed ever so slightly, her disappointment clear as her eyes narrowed just a fraction. "Honestly, I expected more." she said with a note of disapproval. "But to answer your query, you will receive a shortsword of sorts. When the tutorial begins, simply think of the weapon, and it will manifest. However, do keep in mind that your weapon is basic, nothing extraordinary. You'll have to earn greater tools as you progress."

Her response took me by surprise. I hadn't anticipated the mild scolding. Perhaps I had underestimated her expectations of me. Still, I felt my question was necessary, so I stood by it. "Thank you, Miss Oracle. Could you explain the process for securing a patron that aligns with my constitution and overall path?"

The oracle's demeanour shifted ever so slightly. Her previous disappointment seemed to fade, replaced by a glint of satisfaction in her eyes. "Ah, now that is a much better question," she said, her voice laced with approval. "When a mortal selects a class, the deities associated with that class are alerted. But the major deities such as the Olympians or the Aesir were not, This is because your presence is still weak and unstable. The more powerful deities won't take interest in you... At least, not yet. In order to gain a patron, you must first entice a deity. This is something you can earn throughout your time in the tutorial and after you will meet only one of the deities who find you amusing. This will be your chance to impress them and gain their favour. But beware, securing a patron is not the end of your challenges. Should you encounter another potential patron in the future who holds enmity toward your current one, you may be forced to choose between them, sacrificing the blessings of one for the other. The path of patrons is fraught with politics and power struggles."

Her words filled me with both inspiration and dread. It sounded surprisingly easy to initially gain a patron, but the long-term complexities were much more daunting. The idea of juggling relationships with deities and potentially losing their support over rivalries made it clear that this aspect of my journey would require caution and diplomacy. It also explained why the oracle herself, after eight decades of guiding souls, had only one patron. She had navigated these treacherous waters for years.

"Thank you for the clarification," I said, already running potential scenarios through my mind. "In your vast experience, which of my current allies do you recommend I befriend, and which ones should I approach with caution?"

The oracle's reaction to my third question was entirely unexpected. A laugh bubbled up from her chest, full of genuine amusement. Her eyes sparkled with both glee and curiosity as she regarded me. "Hahaha! In all my years of guiding mortals, no one has ever asked for my personal opinion. Can you believe it? They are too focused on themselves, too eager to prove their worth or too frightened to ask. You are quite the interesting one." She paused to collect herself before continuing. "If you truly want my advice, it is this: be cautious of everyone. Trust should be earned, not given freely. Only after you've fought and bled together can you begin to assess who is truly your ally."

Her advice hit home. I'd learned over the years that trust was a fragile thing, easily broken but difficult to rebuild. However, hearing this from the oracle, who had witnessed countless adventurers pass through her realm, reinforced the importance of discretion and careful observation.

"Thank you, Miss Oracle. Your insights are invaluable." I took a moment to reflect on what she had said before posing my final question. "One last thing, if I may. Is it possible for me to bring something from my home to aid me in this one? There's a particular book that might provide me with some valuable insight."

The oracle tilted her head slightly, considering my request. "Hmm, that should be possible," she said after a brief pause. Her caution was fair, and I realised I had been holding on to a small piece of my past, perhaps out of sentimentality. Still, the idea of having something familiar, something comforting, was appealing.

As the book was summoned, the oracle paused to look at the book. Her eyes glowing golden once more, and for a moment I could feel the warmth much like that of a summer day. She then handed the book to me, her eyes now normal.

"Thank you once again, Miss Oracle," I said, bowing slightly in gratitude.

She smiled warmly this time, her earlier sternness having melted away. "Hudson. You seem to have a keen eye and I believe that will serve you well in the trials ahead. The future is bound to be... interesting." Her words were laced with a prophetic undertone, and I couldn't help but feel a chill run down my spine. "Now then.," she continued, "it is time for your tutorial to begin. May the ancient deities of all realms guide you."

With a snap of her fingers, the familiar surroundings of the oracle's chamber dissolved. I was instantly transported to a dense, sprawling forest. The air was thick with the scent of pine and damp earth, and a slight breeze rustled through the trees. As I looked around, I noticed I wasn't alone. Several familiar faces from the selection process were standing nearby, all looking just as disoriented as I felt.

One of the twins broke the silence first. "I suppose we should start with introductions," she said, her voice level but tinged with an underlying tension. "Not like we have a choice anyway. My name is Rebecca, I'm an archer"

Her sister followed suit, speaking in a calm, soothing voice. "I'm Anna, a healer.."

Shawn, who had been lost in his own world, finally spoke up. "My turn," he muttered under his breath before raising his voice. "My name is Shawn. I'm a heavy warrior."

Then, all eyes turned to me. It was my turn to introduce myself. "My name is Hudson, I'm a light warrior." I paused for a moment before continuing. "Now that we've all introduced ourselves we should talk tactics."

Rebecca groaned and rolled her eyes in response "as you can see, anna is a natural support she'll be with me. Shawn is a tank, he'll be upfront. I will climb up high and pick enemies off with my arrows. And as for you, you will just go where needed."

Her analysis was sharp and effective, but I couldn't shake the feeling of being blindsided, like I was just some random extra, standing there without purpose or place.

I didn't appreciate the suspicion. "I'll stick to the vanguard alongside Shawn," I explained. "That's where I'm most effective." This seemed to satisfy her for the moment, and we moved on. At this point Shawn finally looked away from his sword, and raised his hand to speak, but then we heard a sound taking us out of our little meeting.

Beep!
Tutorial has begun.
Current mission: Survive.
Time limit: 29:23:59:52
Survivors: (1000/1000)
May the Ancient Deities of all realms guide you.

The gravity of the situation hit me like a ton of bricks. We were in this for the long haul, and survival was the only objective that mattered now.

Chapter 4: "There is no greater danger than underestimating your opponent." , Lao Tzu

"That's fun," Shawn muttered, his voice dripping with venom.

To clear our minds of the looming danger, I decided to shift the conversation. "Alright, what did everyone learn from their talks with the oracle? We need all the help we can get. I found out some information about our potential patrons." I deliberately chose not to mention the oracle's warnings about distrust; right now, earning their trust was crucial to increasing my chances of survival. Was it selfish? Absolutely. Did I care? Not at all. My priority was to live, even if it meant using these people.

Anna spoke next. She explained how becoming a healer granted her a skill called Lesser Heal as well as knowledge on poisonous plants and medicinal herbs.

Rebecca then explained that her archer class gave her insight into which beasts safe for consumption.

Finally, it was Shawn's turn. "I only asked one question, and I'm glad I did. I found out that we can all become true gods, but it's a little tricky," he explained, filling me with worry. He's far too simple, although that also means I can use him.

"Seriously, that was your question?" I scoffed, having a little fun with this situation.. "Do you even understand the situation we're in? You could've asked about the deities we're supposed to bond with, tips on your class, or how to progress. But instead, you chose to focus on something that almost no one gets?" I needed him to understand the weight of our current situation, before we get the use of it all.

"Can you blame me?" he shot back. "This is an opportunity that we were given. These deities are our greatest gift. Why would I not ask about them?"

Shawn was starting to irritate me. He lacked self respect, yet he already seems fully devoted to unseen deities he only figured out existed. The flames on the hearth flickered lightly, as if to encourage me to be patient and try again. "Listen Shawn, we don't know where we are, we don't know even the basics of what we are trying to do. I just want to get through this alive. To see another day." I glanced at the hearth the twins were sitting around. By the time I looked back it seems that Shawn had somewhat understood giving me enough time to check my card for what the mission was. What I saw was enough to send shivers up my spine.

Current Mission: Survive.
Time Limit: 29:22:24:33
Survivors: 926/1000

We had a brief moment of peace around the hearth, its flickering flames soothing our eyes and ears. A moment of rest was what we finally got, alas it was but a moment. In the silence we heard a rustle through the undergrowth. Hoping it was the wind, yet knowing better, we slowly reached for our weapons, still unsure where the beast, if any, was coming from. Unfortunately it was answered for us, much to our dismay. A grunt echoed to our left and a beast emerged. I looked towards the beast and saw it was a mole-like creature but far larger than any I'd ever seen, the size of a German Shepherd, and it looked far more dangerous. I yelled to get everyone's attention, and prepare for a fight, but I could see the fear in their eyes. A cold sweat ran down my back as I used my *Identify* skill, immediately a small buzz entered my ears, forcing me to focus on the beast more. Which revealed information I wasn't expecting.

Naked Mole Rat. (F⁻)
HP: 590/600

The sight of the creature and the information it revealed made me pray we could work together effectively. Almost instinctively, I noticed Rebecca perched in a tree, firing arrows near the beast's feet, trying to drive it away. Shawn stumbled back, nearly tripping over his own feet as he tried to shield Anna. The beast snarled, undeterred, its eyes gleaming with the anticipation of an easy kill. A sinking feeling told me we were dangerously unprepared for this. My stomach growled, and a reckless idea crossed my mind.

"Rebecca! Is it edible?" I shouted, hoping she could follow my insane plan. She nodded slowly, seemingly understanding my intentions. She aimed for the centre of the beast. Her shot wasn't perfect, but it did the job. The beast, enraged, charged at the base of the oak tree where Rebecca was perched. At that moment, Shawn decided to act. He swung his battle axe with full force at the creature, but the mole rat was quicker than expected, narrowly dodging the blow and causing the axe to embed itself in the tree. The tree shook, making it hard for Rebecca to maintain her balance, let alone shoot.

I had to act. My hands trembled as I slapped the flat of my blade against my leg to grab its attention, the sharp clang echoing in the night. The beast's head snapped toward me, and for a moment, my heart seemed to stop. Every instinct screamed at me to run, but I was rooted to the spot. Now, it was targeting me with all its fury. Rebecca and Shawn understood the situation, with Shawn moving to stand by my side while Rebecca took position on a small rock next to her sister, ready to protect and aid us.

I instructed Shawn to stand his ground and not move too much;I watched Shawn swing with wild desperation, short, frantic strikes that screamed fear more than fury. He wasn't trying to hurt the beast, just push it back, keep it away. All or nothing, that's what he was. And honestly, that made things easier for me.

I charged at the beast, driving my blade into its side. The blade barely penetrated, but the creature whipped around with a savage growl, its fury now directed at me. My breath hitched as I realised I had only succeeded in making myself its primary target. Every muscle in my body screamed to move, but I was frozen for reasons unknown to me. Shawn swung wildly connecting with the beast's hindquarters, the impact sending a sickening jolt up his arms. But the creature barely flinched, turning with a feral snarl as if the pain only fueled its rage. Shawn's eyes widened in panic, he was in over his head, and we both knew it. The beast swiped fiercely at Shawn, sending him flying into the same tree I had thrown him against earlier.

The beast swung at me repeatedly, missing by mere inches each time. It was clear that this creature wasn't a skilled fighter; it was desperate, just like us. My fear began to fade, replaced by excitement. Rebecca's arrows flew, each one barely missing vital points. My heart pounded in my ears, if even one shot went wide, we were done for. As I charged, a single thought consumed me: What if this isn't enough? What if we're outmatched? Rebecca's final arrow pierced the beast's skull, just as I drove my blade into its heart with all the strength I could muster. The creature let out a final, deafening screech before collapsing at our feet. For a long moment, we stood frozen, gasping for breath, the realisation slowly sinking in: We had survived, but only by the skin of our teeth.

As the dust settled, I looked down at my shaking hands, stained with blood, both mine and the beast's. A grin spread across my face, but it wasn't one of triumph. It was the crazed smile of someone who had just danced with death and barely came out alive.

[F]Naked Mole Rat hunted.
Contribution:
Hudson Mitchell 40%
Rebecca Harris 35%
Shawn Adams 25%
Anna Harris 0%
Allocating rewards

Your beginning your fable

Skill Unlocked: Predatorial Vision
This skill is unlocked through analysing your fighting prowess. Predatorial Vision is a heightened sensory ability that allows the user to see and track targets with exceptional clarity and precision, even in challenging environments. When activated, the user's eyesight sharpens, enabling them to perceive subtle movements, heat signatures, and weak points in their prey. This skill also enhances the user's awareness of their surroundings, allowing them to anticipate and react to threats with lightning speed. Whether in low light, dense foliage, or amidst chaotic action, Predatorial Vision ensures that nothing escapes the user's sight, making them a formidable hunter and combatant.

Chapter 5. "There is only one good, knowledge, and one evil, ignorance" , Socrates

At that moment, reality hit me hard. The thrill of battle quickly faded as I grasped the gravity of my rash decision to pursue the hunt. Driven by my own hunger, I disregarded not only my safety but also that of my comrades. I had treated them as mere tools to elevate my own status, ignoring their humanity. But as I saw a blank expression on my healer's face and heard the agonized screams of my fellow warrior, a crucial realization dawned on me. These people are not pawns, not placeholders, they are humans, just like me. And yet, as that thought settled, another followed, unbidden.

I had been careless. Tools must be maintained, not broken prematurely. My hubris had blinded me, leading us to the brink of disaster. The thrill of the hunt had been intoxicating, but now, in the cold light of reality, I saw my slight miscalculation. They were still useful for now. I had no other comparison. They were my only aid and I cannot lose them just yet. I had to put on an act. I prepared myself for a performance of a lifetime

"I... I'm sorry," I stammered. "Rebecca, I made a reckless decision and now look where it's gotten us. You would have made a better choice. We should have scared it away instead of trying to sort out our dinner for a few days."

I tried my best to pull at her heartstrings, hoping that she would agree. But I knew the truth, a part of me still longed to hunt again, driven by instinct. This is dangerous. These thoughts of committing to a hunt. I shouldn't have enjoyed it as much as I did. Alas, here I am.

Shawn snapped me out of my thoughts, slapping my back. "Cut the sappy crap. We barely spoke a word during the fight, and we still came out on top. So stop overthinking and enjoy the spoils."

Rebecca and Anna joined in. "Hudson,," Rebecca began to say, helping to ease my burden. "If we're going to survive this tutorial and beyond, we need to hunt more. Stop beating yourself up, it was necessary."

"To be honest-I was terrified," Anna admitted, yet her expression remained unchanged. "But I agree with my sister. This was a wake-up call. And on the bright side, we all gained something look" strangely after raising an arm showing off her new bracelet she smiled crookedly. Perhaps she was simply trying to better the mood. Perhaps she simply didn't know how to smile. Oh well.

Either way, I felt incredibly grateful at that moment. The situation turned out far better than I could have imagined. I had never been good with people, yet in this twisted scenario, it seemed no one cared about that anymore. It was enough to get by

With that, I decided to check my status to see how much I had grown.

Name: Hudson Mitchell
Rank: Mortal (F)
Class: Light Warrior
Patrons: N/A
Skills:

- **Identify [A]**
- **Low Pain Resistance Level 1 [P]**
- **Predatorial Vision** *(initial)* **[A]**

I also noticed that I gained new boots,boots that for some reason made me feel lighter on my feet and as if I could run forever. With excitement I used my identity thus immediately lowering my mood.

Pretty Fast Boots
These boots were kinda blessed by some Celtic god, probably Lugh's, great great grandchild, a minor god of speed or something. They make you run *a bit* faster than normal, like, you'd probably break a world record if you really tried. Stamina's better too, so you won't get winded as quickly. (*Your Favourite Author*)

The description was sad frankly. I didn't really know what to make of it. Well I guess it is an improvement. I noticed how much easier it was to move around. Yet despite all that, I couldn't help but feel as if I was being watched.

The forest around us felt oppressive, as if the trees themselves were closing in. Every rustle of leaves, every distant howl, set my nerves on edge. We needed to find a safer place, but with every step, I couldn't shake the feeling that we were being watched, haunted by something unseen. Our journey was arduous, to say the least. We travelled for a week, searching for a safe zone, encountering numerous beasts along the way, gaining both injuries and rewards. Finally, after much effort, we found something both hopeful and unsettling: a settlement of other survivors.

But the problem we faced was that we could never agree on what is to come if we are to face survivors. I needed to breach this topic, if not now we would be blindsided by any possibility of deceit.

"Guys," I began, "what are we going to do if we meet other survivors?"

"Uh we talk?" Shawn responded with his incredible intelligence.

"I mean clearly we need one of us to take charge." Anna said "to lead negotiations" Anna became more and more open as this tutorial went on. She shuffled less, and became more comfortable with the rest of us. But I still can't trust any of them.

"I'll do it" rebecca added

"Why?" I asked

"I mean clearly I'm the best option." she began "Anna just got out of her shell. And as if I would trust you or Shawn." There was venom behind her voice when mentioned Shawn and I. Clearly something more than what we did. It was better not to press it. So I told Shawn to drop it before he tried butting in.

So with that discussed it was decided that Rebecca would lead the negotiations. Our trust in each other had grown during our expedition, as you might imagine. We relied on each other in combat and strategy, though none of us ever shared personal information. Our trust was based on survival, and perhaps that was for the best.

It was at this point we saw a gate of some sorts, a little makeshift stronghold. There was a guard standing there waiting for our arrival. So without further ado we made our presence known.

"Halt! State your names and intentions!" A rugged man, standing about six feet tall and clad in heavy armour, greeted us at the gate. It was clear that everyone here had endured their own struggles during this tutorial, which explained their wariness toward strangers. Given the current state of affairs, this was only natural.

Mission: Survive.
Time Limit: 20:13:28:34
Survivors: 434/1000

The tutorial's situation was dire, less than ten days in, and over half of the participants had already perished. Rebecca stepped forward for introductions. "Good afternoon. My name is Rebecca, an archer as you can see. This is my party, we have two warriors and a healer. We're seeking a safe place to stay." She kept the introduction brief, earning her a nod of approval from myself. Delving more than necessary information is asking for trouble.

The rugged man replied, "I'm Michael, a guard here. We'll take you to our leader to see if the warriors have any use." Alarm bells went off in my head as I noticed he didn't mention the twins. Two possibilities crossed my mind, one of which I didn't particularly like.

As we were being escorted, I noticed how large the settlement was, there were countless eyes staring at us, as if we were freaks of nature. These people felt off, the 20 or so tents had no individuality from each other. The settlement did not feel homely. It felt unnatural. Designed to make you comply. It reminded me of *that place*.

We were escorted to a tent in the centre of the settlement. A tent different from the rest, larger, more imposing with more fauna surrounding it. Clearly the tent of the ruler. In this tent we were greeted by a short, nimble man. "Well, isn't this nice, more survivors? Come in, make yourselves comfortable. My name is Jacob, I'm an Orator. I know it's a rare class; I think I'm the only one in the tutorial. How else would I have managed to lead such a fine group of people?"

Something was off. I didn't trust him. My instincts screamed that he was lying, but I couldn't immediately figure out why. I scanned the room for clues. On his belt hung two karambit blades, short and deadly. A makeshift bullseye on the wall was filled with holes far too large to be made by darts. A bottle of viscous purple fluid sat on his desk. Something wasn't right, this orator was more than he seemed, far too ready for war. But I didn't know enough yet.

This man was more than just dangerous, he was calculating, cunning, the type who would turn on you the moment it suited his plans. A nagging sense of doom settled in my gut. Something was bound to go wrong, and when it did, I feared it would be catastrophic. My pulse pounded in my ears, each beat a reminder of how close we were to disaster. As Rebecca spoke, my mouth went dry, and I could feel a cold sweat breaking out along my spine. Every word felt like a step closer to a precipice, where one wrong move could send us all plummeting. He responded, "Of course, a healer and an archer of such... stature are rare in these lands. You'll both have a place to stay, Don't you worry" he said with a sly grin. " As for you two, unfortunately we have more than enough warriors, you are not needed. Good luck." he explains, leaning back, focusing on the twins once more. The guards, as if by habit were ushering us whilst showing us to the door.

I was certain now. The look in his eyes revealed his true intentions. While I was confident Rebecca could handle herself, this situation was far from ideal. Splitting up our party wasn't just a risk, it was a death sentence. The thought of leaving Rebecca and Anna behind made my stomach churn, but hesitation now would be fatal. I had to act, and fast, to protect my allies from a fate they didn't even see coming.

"We will earn our place. Give us a task. You will see how valuable we are.." I glared at Jacob, no longer cared for any semblance of respect; this man didn't deserve it. But I had to prioritise my allies' safety.

After my demand, something in jacob switched. He finally looked at us as if we were more than just another number. He looks at us, slowly leaning forward. The guards retreated without an order, and that's when he opened his mouth.

"You know, many like you have come before. Men whose hubris clouded their judgement. Every one of them was given the same hunt, and none returned. Do you really want to take that risk?" I forced myself to nod at Jacob's remark, my jaw clenched so tight it ached. Doubt gnawed at me, was this a trap? Were we walking into a death sentence? But there was no turning back now; I had to project confidence, even if I was far from certain "Very well. Ten miles west of here, there's a creature known as the Predator of the Plains. We know little about it. Our scouts tried to identify it, but all they got were question marks. Do you believe the two of you can handle that? If so, I'll gladly set up a tent for you." without so much of a nod, shawn and i accepted the wager, leaving the settlement not knowing if we were to return

As we set out, the settlement faded into the distance, replaced by the vast, unforgiving wilderness. Every step felt like a march toward doom, and I couldn't shake the feeling that this challenge would test more than just our strength; it would test our very souls. The Predator of the Plains awaited, and with it, the shadow of death loomed ever closer.

Chapter 6. "He who has a reason to live for, can bear almost any how." , Nietzsche

Shawn's POV:

I understood his anger, Hudson's that is. He didn't speak much but I could tell that he was a good person at heart. He didn't like it when people hurt those he cared for. And I am the same way. I was angry at being ripped from those who I considered family. I was angry at being in this situation to begin with. But even thorns have roses. This situation gave me an opportunity. An opportunity for all of us. The gods gifted us all equipment after the first hunt. All of us got something out of it. Although Rebecca didn't take it since it was 'pathetic', we were gifted something through their grace. And the strongest of us all was this young man by me. Together we will slay this beast, begin our legend and perhaps even get another gift. Yet despite all the potential gains, my anger was not soothed.

I was livid, not at Hudson, but at that damned orator. I saw the look in his eyes. As a father to a daughter, my blood boiled at the very thought of his schemes. If it hadn't been for Hudson's quick intervention, we would've been dead on the spot. Now, survival was all we had left. As we trekked onward, the air grew thick with tension, every rustle in the underbrush setting my nerves on edge.

Then I saw it, a monstrous beast, it had three heads, a grotesque amalgamation of lion, goat, and serpent. My blood ran cold as its gaze locked onto us, a predator sizing up its prey. Its body loomed over us, as large as a Leopard 2A7 tank. I heard a faint whisper from Hudson beside me, "Fuck, it's a chimaera."

I didn't know much about the beast, but I'd seen depictions of it in the book Hudson occasionally read. Naturally, Hudson took the lead. He ordered me to focus on the beast's heads while he handled the rear. I understood why. I was stronger but less agile than Hudson, and I couldn't afford to be poisoned by the serpent's fangs. I used my identify skill on the beast to grasp its ferocity.

Predator of the Plains
Infant Chimera (Learned) D$^+$
HP: 9880/10000

Hudson and I exchanged glances, a silent understanding passing between us. We were in over our heads, and we both knew it. For the first time, doubt crept into my mind, were we really strong enough to take this thing down? The thought of failure, of dying here, so far from my family, chilled me to the bone.

We assumed our positions, bracing for the fight of our lives. I'd like to say that aligning ourselves with our strengths made the battle easier, but it didn't. Every strike from the chimaera sent shockwaves through my body, my arms trembling from the force. The relentless assault battered not just my defences, but my spirit. Each parry felt like I was holding back a tidal wave with nothing but a broken shield, and with every second, the weight of the battle crushed me a little more. I knew Hudson would deal the most damage, with only one head targeting him, while I had to fend off two. I couldn't dodge, so I defended, standing my ground and silently praying for Hudson to pull through.

The beast roared in pain, and I was momentarily confused. All my strikes had been superficial at best. Then I felt a slimy, viscous mass land on my neck. Ignoring it, I swung with all my might, trying to capitalise on the beast's shock. I managed to leave a deep gash in the goat head's neck, but then we received a system warning.

Beep!
The Infant Chimera used Unique Skill: Berserk
Strength and Agility increased by 50%
Unable to feel pain.

The chimaera's berserk state unleashed a fury that was beyond anything I had imagined. It attacked with the ferocity of a storm, and I was nothing more than a leaf in its path. The blow sent me flying, crashing into the ground with such force that I felt the air rush out of my lungs. Pain seared through my body, and as I struggled to rise, I realised with horror that I might not be able to stand again. I was fortunate not to be bleeding, but my broken bones weren't helping. All I could do was watch in horror as the battle between the beast and my friend continued.

Hudson roared, drawing the beast's attention. He must have noticed my predicament. The beast lunged at him, and I saw something both breathtaking and terrifying, Hudson narrowly dodging each blow, but now there were only 2 heads, Hudson must have decapitated the serpent. As I lay on the ground, struggling to breathe, I caught a glimpse of Hudson. His eyes, once sharp and focused, had turned pitch black, like the void itself had seeped into his soul. A chill ran down my spine, but it wasn't just fear, it was something deeper, a primal instinct warning me that whatever Hudson had become, it was something terrifyingly powerful, something that might one day turn on us all. But what was even more unsettling was the way his style shifted entirely, from defence to a more aggressive approach. It was as if the change in his eyes unleashed a primal force within him.

He allowed the goat's horns to impale him slightly, using the leverage to rip off the goat head while simultaneously swinging his blade at the lion. It was a strategy no ordinary human could pull off. It was like watching two apex predators battle for dominance. Only then did I realise my own shortcomings.

I had always been set in my ways, never adapting or changing my methods because they had never failed me since the mole rat. But witnessing Hudson's adaptability in battle made me realise I needed to do the same. I had to become unpredictable yet efficient. I might not fight like Hudson, but I could still find my own path.

With only one head remaining, the young chimaera used its final chance to attack Hudson. It leaped, maw wide open, aiming to end the fight in one swift blow. But that was its biggest mistake. Hudson, bloodied and barely standing, raised his blade in a move that defied all logic. It wasn't just a strike, it was the culmination of everything he had become, a blow delivered with precision and a ruthless determination that left no room for doubt. The chimaera leaped, its jaws wide, and in that split second, time seemed to freeze. Hudson's blade found its mark, piercing through flesh and bone with a finality that echoed in the silence that followed. The blade pierced deep into the chimaera's gaping mouth, and I noticed his eyes were still a deep, unnerving black. A moment of silence, then a system message.

Beep!
Predator of the Plains hunted.

Contribution:
Hudson Mitchell 65%
Shawn Adams 35%
Allocating Rewards...

Skill Unlocked: *Defensive Fortitude:*
A passive skill that enhances the user's ability to withstand physical and magical attacks. When activated, this skill significantly boosts the user's resilience, allowing them to endure prolonged battles without succumbing to exhaustion or injury. The longer the user remains in combat, the more effective this skill becomes, gradually increasing defence stats over time. Ideal for tank roles or front-line fighters expected to absorb damage and protect allies. Strength +5%, Incoming Damage -5%.

Satisfied with my new skill, I opened my status.

Name: Shawn Adams
Rank: Mortal (F)
Class: Heavy Warrior
Patron #1: N/A
Patron #2: N/A
Patron #3: N/A

Skills:
- **Identify [A]**
- **Defensive Fortitude Level 1 [P]**

As I took in the new stats, I noticed Hudson walking toward me, still smiling despite the exhaustion and wounds. As Hudson approached, his eyes returning to normal, I felt a surge of relief, but it was tainted by a dark undercurrent of fear. What had I just witnessed? The man who had saved my life was also the man who, for a moment, had become something else entirely. Gratitude warred with unease in my heart, leaving me uncertain of what the future held. He lay down beside me, healing slowly. I wondered how many skills he had gained in that fight but chose to dismiss it. After all, this man was the reason I was still alive.

Chapter 7. "Strife is justice; rage brings forth the strength and necessity for change." , Heraclitis

Hudson POV:

The battle was both excruciatingly painful and exhilarating. From the moment it began, Shawn and I had to use every skill in our arsenal to slay the beast. Without Shawn's help, I know I would have failed. He played his role perfectly, and it surprised me to see him looking at me with newfound inspiration. I hoped that my fight had given him a few ideas on how to pursue his own path.

It seemed after enough battles, one could naturally regenerate. Shawn stared at me in shock as he watched my minor cuts heal themselves. Unfortunately, the larger wounds inflicted by the goats required external help to stop the bleeding.

It was then that Shawn broke the silence. "Yo, Hudson. How are we supposed to carry this beast back to the settlement?" I laughed, not because of the question itself, but because I hadn't even considered Jacob calling us liars when we returned with the news. So, we did what had to be done.

Since Shawn's strength stat was higher than mine, he became our impromptu porter, dragging the beast's corpse back with us. Of course, I wasn't so shameless as to let him do all the work.

I carried the heads. The journey back was relatively smooth, though incredibly tiring and arduous due to the 12-ton weight we were dragging.

Michael stood at the gate, his figure stiff and unnatural, like a sentinel guarding a terrible secret. His eyes flicked to the beast behind us, widening in a mix of disbelief and dread.

"You're not supposed to be alive," he stammered, his voice filled with fear. He glanced between us and then noticed the hulking mass behind us, his eyes widening with terror. Jacob was hiding something, something that would incite our rage. Michael charged at us with desperation, clearly intent on hiding whatever secret the settlement was keeping. Shawn and I exchanged a glance, knowing we were thinking the same thing. I was Michael's target. He must have thought I would hesitate since I had never killed before. He was only half right. Without hesitation, I swung my blade toward his neck, decapitating him in a single motion my blade tore through his neck effortlessly, flesh stretching, bone cracking as his head became weightless under my blade, his face still crumpled with desperation, a nightmarish expression as it rolled against the dirt. His body folded in on itself, his sword slapped against my shoulder weightlessly, the sound cracking in the air. Blood spurting from the stump of his head pooling into the dirt staining it black. His eyes twitched absently as his head rolled to a standstill. A deafening silence filled the air, time froze.

I had just killed a man.

My thoughts were in turmoil. I had just killed a man, a man who was probably just doing his job. But he pointed his blade at me; he wanted to hide something from me, from us. That didn't change the fact that I had committed a sin. A deep, gnawing fear coiled within me, a beast of its own, threatening to consume my resolve. But I couldn't afford to falter, not now. Not with the storm of chaos I could feel looming just over the horizon. I didn't hesitate; it felt natural, as if it was the best solution. I didn't even attempt to reason. But the worst part was that this wouldn't end with one death. I could no longer rely on reason, even though I knew that's what I should do. Today was the start of a war, and even though I didn't start it, I had to finish it. I was a murderer.

As I stood frozen, Shawn shook me back to my senses. Shawn's hand tightened on his weapon, his knuckles white. "Hudson…" His voice was steady, but there was a flicker of something, fear, determination, just beneath the surface. "We have to do this. You know it as well as I do." I looked into his eyes and saw that despite his fear, there was a steely resolve, a courage to continue down the path of war. We weren't prepared for this, but we had to steel ourselves for what was to come.

We ran inside, trying to gather our bearings. At first, everything seemed normal, but something was unsettling. The camp was unsettlingly quiet, as if the very air had thickened with anticipation.

The usual clamour of voices and laughter had died away, replaced by a heavy, oppressive silence. It was as if the camp was no longer filled with empowered individuals but rather with ordinary humans.

This caused both Shawn and me to slow down. While I hoped for a peaceful resolution, we both knew it wasn't possible, so we decided to walk around and gather clues.

"Maybe they know where the twins are?" Shawn suggested.

"Right now, they only know that we're a party." At this point I thought about all the knowledge I gained, and then as if by the will of the gods who were watching an idea came to me, "Have you ever heard of the Trojan horse?" I didn't know at this point, but a smile slowly crept on my face.

Shawn reluctantly nodded, probably because he couldn't see a better option. Much to our surprise, however, Jacob approached us silently. I hadn't even sensed him. He slowly opened his mouth.

Before we even braced ourselves for our crazy plan, a figure approached and I froze.

"I expected nothing less from you," he said, clapping slowly as his eyes rested on my stained sword. "I take it Michael's dead? useless buffoon, probably would have claimed the kills for himself" he chuckled as he approached. "Now, time to see your party members? a deals a deal" he says, taking control immediately.

Jacob was clever. He had anticipated our plans and made countermeasures in advance. If both of us went along with him now, we'd be dancing in the palm of his hand, a truly fearsome foe. To throw him off track, I had to play a dangerous card. I had already planted the seed of the plan in Shawn's mind, but I silently prayed that he saw the genius behind my madness.

"Never said I needed those bitches?" Shawn whipped his head, Jacob raised an eyebrow in response. But I don't need to play by his rules, "We were basically strangers two weeks ago, did you really think that we are a family? They aren't your daughters either." I needed him to play along, he knew I had my plan, let's just pray he understood it.

"You and I have a lot to chat about, let Shawn grab the kids." I then held up my stained blade, letting it rest on my shoulder, as I slowly moved towards jacob, "i'm getting good at hunting, last i checked, there's a job opening." Jacob stared down at me and the longer he stared the more my facade became reality.

I hoped the man who claimed he was an orator was arrogant enough to believe me, to think he could manipulate me into doing his bidding. Time seemed to stretch as I waited, each second a lifetime. Jacob's face remained impassive, unreadable. At least until the corner of his mouth twitched into a small, knowing grin. The game had just begun.

"I suppose we do need to chat, hudson" I smiled, knowing I had never given him my name, another reason to be cautious "okay grandpa go get the kids," He waved at his subordinates, dismissing them. The stage was set

Beep!
A certain goddess is displeased with your plan but acknowledges it.
A certain god is laughing with curiosity, eager to see how your plan unfolds.

A shiver ran down my spine as the message appeared, the goddess's disapproval like a cold whisper against my skin. I now knew that I was being watched, and that even some of the gods understood my plan. As I followed Jacob as we entered a tent, taking a seat across from him, a hand of mine clenched under the table holding my leg still. Jacob sat, leaned back comfortably as he eyed me. I knew I had to use every survival skill I had to make this work. High stakes as usual, nothing I hadn't dealt with before these trials. I leaned forwards studying him. Seeing my reflection in him, the no man's land between us, a wordless struggle for powerAfter what felt like an eternity we heard a loud crash

Jacob quickly addressed me with a smile. "It seems your friend is far more loyal than I assumed. He's causing me some trouble. What do you say? Do you want to kill your old accomplice for a better one?"

I paused for a few seconds before responding. "Right," I said leaning back " I'm not taking orders from a fraud, you have not impressed the gods, did you honestly think you impressed me?"I scoffed.

Jacob was stunned for a moment, and before he could summon his guards, I grabbed him by the throat, my grip tightening with every word, feeling the pulse of his fear beneath my fingers. I could feel the anger simmering, rising with every breath, but I kept it controlled, a weapon to be unleashed at the right moment.
"How stupid do you think I am, Jacob?" My voice was low, almost calm, but beneath it was a current of barely restrained rage. "I've seen the way you look at them… like they're trophies to be collected, not people." I leaned in closer, my voice dropping to a dangerous whisper. "You never even bothered to hide your intentions, did you? Thought you could manipulate us, use us like pawns in your little game."

Each word dripped with venom, my fury boiling just beneath the surface, threatening to spill over."And you know what? That's what pisses me off the most." I squeezed tighter, watching the fear flicker in his eyes, feeding the fire within me. "You're arrogant, Jacob. Arrogant enough to think you could control us. Me" I felt the rage surging, but I forced myself to stay focused, to use it as fuel. "But you've underestimated me. I'm not just some pawn in your game, I'm the one who's going to end it."

I could see his hand trembling as he reached for his knife. My other hand shot out, grabbing his wrist with a crushing force. "You really thought you could stab me, didn't you? Pathetic." The words were spat out, sharp and cold, a reflection of the fury building inside.

I leaned in even closer, "Now listen to me, and listen well, because these are the last words you'll ever hear." My voice was a deadly calm, the kind that comes before a storm tears everything apart. "I'm going to kill you, Jacob. And then, I'm going to walk out of here with my party, and there's nothing you or your men can do to stop me. If anyone tries to get in our way…" I let the threat hang in the air, the promise of violence unspoken but clear. "This won't be a hunt, Jacob. It won't even be a war. It'll be a massacre, and I'll make sure every last one of them knows it was you who brought it upon them."

My eyes locked onto his, and I saw the terror there, but I didn't care. The last shred of control slipped from my grasp as I crushed his throat with a final, brutal squeeze, the snap of cartilage like the crack of thunder heralding the storm to come. But even as the rage consumed me, I knew this was just the beginning. The plan wasn't over, and I wasn't done. Not yet.

Beep!
Sub-Mission: War against Earth Tutorial Settlement.
Pass: Upgraded armour.
Failure: Death.
[May the ancient deities of all realms guide you.]

Chapter 8. "I am not what happened to me, I am what I choose to become." , Carl Jung.

Rebecca POV:

I've always distrusted men. No, it's more accurate to say I've learned that men cannot be trusted. The real reason I chose the archer class had nothing to do with my physical ability. It was because I couldn't trust anyone to watch my back, not even for a moment. Being summoned to the tutorial felt like both a curse and a blessing. But at least I had my sister. She's always been my protector, my anchor, and I love her for it.

She inherited all the good qualities from our late mother, who was a true angel among people. Our mother shielded us from the monster we shared our DNA with. That man wasn't human. I doubt anyone else could empathise with our struggles. He was a monster in human flesh. Maybe that's why it was easy for me to kill monsters in the tutorial. Killing them was like purging the world of his memory, one arrow at a time.

The memory seared into my mind like a brand, the air thick with the stench of alcohol and sweat… and blood. England lost the 2018 semi-finals, but we lost something far more precious that night, our mother's spirit. We were just 13, but that night… that night, I learned what true fear was. The kind that wraps around your heart and squeezes until you can't breathe. We watched in silence as the empty bottles piled up.

The tension in the air was suffocating, pressing down on us like a heavy, dark cloud. He ordered our mother into a room, and the door closed like a prison gate. Her screams pierced the air, each one a dagger that tore into my soul. We huddled together, the walls closing in around us, her agony stretching on for hours, ripping her apart piece by piece… and with her, our innocence. I felt something inside me break that night; a fragile hope, shattered beyond repair. From that day, something changed in the way Mother looked at us. She no longer feigned happiness. She became a husk of her former self, yet she still protected us as much as she could. Until she couldn't. The day we found her… her body wasn't just lifeless, it was broken, drained, a hollow shell that once housed the woman who had given everything to protect us. The smell of death clung to the air, a cruel reminder of the life she had endured, and the monster who had destroyed her. When the man who called himself our father saw what had happened, he blamed us.

We became the new targets of our father's insanity. Anna, my courageous sister, came up with a plan to escape. She led us to freedom when we were sixteen, but the scars never left us. We met a man who offered us refuge, and we lived with him for three years, until the tutorial began. Those were happy years for me, a brief respite from the storm.

But I didn't realise then that Anna was slowly beginning to resemble our mother. I was too naive, too eager to believe in a happy ending, to see the signs. But when we teleported to the white room, she was crying. The truth spilled out, and with it, a flood of regret that threatened to drown me. I regretted not seeing it sooner. I used one of my questions to uncover the truth, which only made my heart break further. That's why I chose the bow, I vowed never to let anyone else hurt my sister.

Now, I have to live with the consequences of my actions. As soon as the men left, I asked about Jacob's true intentions. His honesty was a knife to my heart, twisting deeper with every word. Fear overtook me, and before I could react, one of his men incapacitated me from behind. Now I find myself in a tent, tied up, with my sister unconscious beside me. I hate men. I hate their lies, their betrayal, their cruelty. Hudson and Shawn probably are worse. How else are they so strong? Even if they come back. I will never let them close.

As I desperately tried to form an escape plan, my mind raced, fragments of trauma crashing into my thoughts, threatening to overwhelm me. The tent flap opened, and my body tensed, every muscle coiled like a spring ready to snap. A familiar figure entered, but instead of relief, I felt a surge of anger. I couldn't afford to trust him, I couldn't afford to trust anyone.

"Rebecca, Anna, I'm here to get you out. Hudson has a mad plan. He's starting a massacre, and I don't think we'll be able to stop him. Let's get out of here before anything begins," Shawn explained, his voice laced with urgency. His words were like venom, each one fueling the fire in my chest. I wanted to believe him, to see a saviour in his worried eyes, but all I could feel was the boiling rage, the helplessness of years past surging to the surface. Men lie. They always lie. I wasn't going to be their victim again. I needed proof. I needed to ignite the flames of war myself.

"Give me your knife," I snarled, the words sharp, almost feral. The cold edge of desperation sliced through my resolve, but I couldn't show weakness. I needed control. I needed to feel that cold steel in my hands, a promise that this time, it would be me who decides. "'I'll knock you out and escape." The words were a lifeline, a way to reclaim the power that had been stolen from me. "I can't hear any screams so there is no war happening. Give me the knife. Prove you're on my side." My gaze bore into him, daring him to defy me, to show his true colours. He looked at me with concern but eventually obliged. He didn't argue, didn't hesitate, a wise choice. After cutting both Anna's and my ropes and grabbing my gear, I stayed true to my word. It seemed Shawn had his own plans, he moved like a man possessed, hurling himself into the tent's supports. The entire structure groaned under the force, and with a deafening crash, the tent collapsed around us, the world falling into chaos. I didn't pause to think. I grabbed Anna and ran, the instinct to survive pounding in my veins like a war drum.

I didn't wait for him to recover. I half-dragged, half-carried my sister, her body heavy and limp as she slowly stirred, her groggy eyes trying to focus. I didn't have time for gentleness. "Anna, get up! We're not dying here!" The urgency in my voice was fueled by the thought of losing her, of failing her again. As we climbed onto the rock, I felt the weight of years of pain and fear clawing at my insides. It exploded out of me in a scream that tore at my throat, the sound of a soul pushed to its breaking point. 'YOU OFFERED US SAFETY!' The words ripped through the night, filled with a fury that had been building for far too long. 'YOU GAVE US YOUR WORD! NOW WE WILL HAVE OUR REVENGE!' The rage was a living thing now, untamable, and it surged forward, driving me to knock an arrow and unleash it into the crowd below. Each shot was a release, each scream from the crowd a twisted satisfaction. The fury in my voice was a living thing, raw and uncontainable, ready to consume everything in its path. I looked down at the mob, their faces filled with both horror and rage. Their fear only fueled my anger, stoking the flames higher. I knocked an arrow into my bow and fired into the crowd. I didn't care for accuracy, my wrath didn't need to be precise. With a crowd this size, my arrow was bound to find a target. And then it happened:

Beep!
A goddess is incredibly impressed with your resolve.

The notification was a distant hum in the back of my mind, overshadowed by the bloodlust surging through my veins. As I continued firing, I noticed out of the corner of my eye a familiar figure with blood dripping from his fingertips. He was a spectre of death, cloaked in makeshift armour, a short sword glimmering in the moonlight. He looked in my direction, his deep black eyes sending a shiver of fear down my spine. But then he smiled, a dark, knowing smile that spoke of shared vengeance, of an unspoken bond in our desire for retribution. In his eyes, I saw the same fire that burned in my own vengeance, pure and unyielding. It wasn't just support he was offering; it was a shared promise, a pact forged in blood and fury. I would accept it, and together, we would burn this place to the ground, leaving nothing but ashes in our wake.

Chapter 9 "The essence of all warfare is destruction." , Arthur Schopenhauer.

Hudson's POV:

I slowly emerged from the tent, each step heavy with the weight of my own transformation. Dread coiled within me like a living thing, but I forced it down, steeling myself with the cold resolve of what had to be done. The blood dripping from my fingertips felt like a physical manifestation of the darkness seeping into my soul. My gaze wandered, almost unwillingly, to the source of the commotion. My breath hitched as my eyes locked onto the twins, both battered and bruised, their garments torn in a way that sent a jolt of terror through me. The thought that someone might have taken advantage of the chaos, that they had been assaulted, made my blood run cold. All my doubt, all my regret, melted away in that moment, replaced by a burning rage that ignited every fibre of my being.

I forced myself to analyse their injuries, my mind a ruthless machine despite the storm raging inside me. I needed to ensure they could survive, to reassure myself that they were still with me, still breathing. My lips curled into a small, almost unnatural smile, a futile attempt to offer them courage when I had none left for myself.

But there was no time for hesitation, no time to process the horror that had been inflicted upon them. I threw back my head and unleashed a deafening roar, a primal cry that shattered the night and made the crowd slowly turn their heads towards me. With a devilish grin twisting my features, I charged into what could very well be my final battle.

Predatorial Vision was a marvel, a cruel gift that slowed time to a crawl, forcing me to witness every grotesque detail of the slaughter. As I plunged into the enemy ranks, the world around me seemed to warp, each movement hyper-focused, each strike a calculated effort to stay alive. But my fighting style wasn't about survival, it was about destruction. Most sought the most effective victory; I craved the quickest, the most brutal. My movements were like a deranged dance on a tightrope, where one misstep would send me plummeting into the abyss. The enemies were weak, but their numbers were overwhelming, a tide of bodies that threatened to drown me.

Parrying blows would waste precious time, so I let the minor strike land, each cut a reminder of my humanity, of the fragility I despised. Every swing of my blade brought down another foe, the resistance of flesh against steel barely registering anymore. I was relieved that the army focused on me, a perverse gratitude that allowed Rebecca to pick off the enemies with little difficulty. But for every enemy slain, two more took their place.

The battle was endless, a suffocating nightmare of blood and screams, and the excitement I once felt slowly gave way to a deep, gnawing despair. I was drowning in the blood of my enemies, and the realisation twisted something inside me. But I knew, I knew, these people were in the same predicament. Nothing is more terrifying than a single being capable of slaughtering dozens of men. I needed help. I needed support.

As if by some cruel miracle, my final party member entered the fray, flanking the army from the east. The enemy forces split, but it didn't bring the relief I so desperately needed. Vultures circled above, their presence a grim omen of death, a reminder of the end that awaited me. I wanted to give in, to let the abyss swallow me whole. My muscles screamed with every swing, my eyes burned with every passing second, and the manic grin that had once felt natural now began to falter, cracking under the weight of reality. The pain was almost unbearable. Then, as if by divine intervention, the pain suddenly vanished.

Beep!
You have been blessed by a Healer.

Another miracle, another thread of hope in the darkness. The pain was gone, but the fatigue remained, a leaden weight dragging me down. With every passing moment, my body slowed, each movement becoming more laborious, more strained. I had no choice, I risked everything, fueling myself with instinct, temporarily forgetting who I was. "17…18…19" I counted, the words a lifeline in the chaos, the only thing keeping me from spiralling into complete madness.

A laugh escaped my lips, a hollow, bitter sound. With every swing, I descended further into madness, a downward spiral of destruction.

Beep!

I ignored the message, its importance drowned out by the overpowering need to destroy, to kill. The only thing that mattered now was the annihilation of anything that moved. I didn't care who, anyone alive was a threat, a target for the wrath that consumed me. I saw everything. The deeper I plunged into their ranks, the stronger the enemies became. To think I had struggled with mere pawns, how laughable. I was better than this. I was better than all of them!

My madness consumed me, sharpening my vision until the world around me crystallised into a grotesque clarity. It was as if my mind had transcended the frailties of the flesh, granting me a sinister understanding of the battlefield's rhythm.

Every breath, every slight shift in the air, every twitch of muscle fibre became a vivid prelude to the inevitable strike. They thought their feints could deceive me, but I saw through them as if they were moving through treacle, their intentions laid bare like an open book. I anticipated their every move, my perception slicing through the fog of war with razor precision.

I could see the fear in their eyes, masked behind bravado. How laughable it was, their futile attempts to best me, to corner me, to defeat the man I had become. A low chuckle escaped my lips, tinged with a madness that echoed in my skull like a deranged symphony. How dare they think they could stop me? Me? I am Hudson Mitchell, being far superior to them, an apex predator among feeble prey. I revelled in the carnage, the chaos, in the way their blades sang past me, unable to touch what they could no longer understand.

But with each victorious strike, with each laugh that echoed from my blood-streaked mouth, something twisted deeper within me. My madness, so potent, so exhilarating, began to metastasize, warping the very essence of my being. The clarity that had once been my weapon now fractured, splintering into a thousand shards of discordant thought. The battlefield around me became a shifting nightmare, figures distorting into grotesque spectres. My enemies no longer had faces, only grinning skulls that mocked me with every swing of their swords.

I should have known. I should have seen that in my delusion of grandeur, in my belief in my own invincibility, I had sealed my fate. Their swords, once slow and predictable, now moved with the speed of nightmares. They struck from every direction, piercing through my defences, drawing blood, but it felt like they were slicing through something far more profound than flesh. Each wound was not just a physical pain, but a tear in the fabric of my sanity, a reminder that I was not invincible, that my mind was a labyrinth from which I could no longer escape.

My laughter grew shrill, a cackle that clawed its way out of my throat, uncontrollable, hysterical. I was slashed, stabbed, torn apart piece by piece, but I could not stop. I could not surrender to the reality that had slipped from my grasp. Every movement became a grotesque dance of futility, my body moving as if on strings pulled by some cruel, unseen puppeteer. The madness that had once been my strength now drove me into the abyss, and yet, even as I felt the life drain from me, I continued to fight. I continued to laugh.

For in the end, it wasn't the swords that killed me. It was the madness, the very madness that had granted me vision, that had stripped away the illusions of normalcy, only to replace them with a darker, more terrifying truth. A truth that devoured me whole, leaving nothing behind but a hollow shell, still clinging to the delusion that it had ever been superior to anything at all.

And then, as if the storm had passed, a bitter clarity returned, washing over me like icy water. The battle raged on, but I was no longer the unstoppable force I had believed myself to be. I was angry, not at the settlement, not at the enemies that now encircled me like vultures, but at myself. How could I have been so arrogant? How could I have forgotten the most fundamental truth of all,how could I forget that I, too, could die?

In that moment, I made a decision; a desperate, final grasp at sanity. I decided to retreat, to step back from the chaos, if only for a breath, for a single moment to regain my composure. I needed to breathe. The madness had consumed me, but now I needed to find something solid, something real, to hold onto. As I stepped back, the bigger picture came into focus, and what I saw horrified me. I had forgotten the very reason I had entered this battlefield. I had come here with a purpose, a mission, but somewhere in the depths of my insanity, that purpose had been swallowed whole.

I glanced at my party, the comrades who had fought alongside me, who had trusted me. Regret hit me like a physical blow. How could I have been so blinded by my own ego, my own madness? I had never once thought to support them, to fight for them as they had fought for me. What kind of monster was I becoming?

The battlefield, once teeming with enemies, now held fewer than ten. But the sight of them no longer filled me with the thrill of the hunt. Instead, I felt a weakness envelop my body, my knees buckling as I collapsed to the ground. A bitter laugh escaped me, a hollow echo of the manic cackles that had once filled the air. I laughed at myself, wondering how I had let it get this bad, how I had lost sight of everything, how I had let the madness consume me so completely.

It hadn't been this low even against the Chimaera, a foe I had faced with courage, with purpose. Now, I was a shadow of the warrior I had been, brought low not by the swords of my enemies, but by the madness that had once been my weapon. The madness that had become my downfall.

The pain washed over me in an agonising wave, crashing through me like a relentless tide. I couldn't comprehend what my body was going through. It was as if I was bathing in the fiery river of Phlegethon, each drop searing my flesh, burning me from the inside out. I felt the acid in my stomach creeping out of its walls, burning my intestines. My bones shook, my vision blurred, and it felt like the weight of the world was pressing on my eyelids. I saw my comrades rushing towards me, worry etched across their faces. They were only halfway to me when I finally succumbed to the darkness.

When I awoke, the world felt distant, muffled as if I were submerged underwater. I was told I had been out for 20 minutes. Twenty minutes, long enough for my reality to shatter, to reform in ways I couldn't yet understand. I looked around and saw a horde of corpses surrounding me. The stench of death was suffocating, a sickening reminder of the madness that had claimed me. A glowing light emanated from near my chest. I looked up at the tear-streaked face it belonged to.

"Thank you, Anna," I said, my voice barely a whisper. "It's okay now."

"They're dead hudson. Of course it's ok now" anna said flatly "why even bother... Why do all this? what for?" she asked indifferently as she healed.

"What are you talking about? We're a team, we did this to survive, for all of us to survive," he said trying to convince himself more than us "And look!" he said pointing to the spoils. handing them out. "This is our life now, we have to survive... we have to."

Anna just nodded slightly to Shawn's remark, still silent, her thoughts a thousand miles away. Rebecca, on the other hand, stared at us with a mix of both anger and acknowledgment. At that moment, I realised I had never truly understood the twins. There was a lot hiding behind those eyes. We were only alive out of necessity for them. I had to remind myself not to get too personal with them. A sound from the system pulled me from my darkening thoughts.

Beep!
Hidden mission successful!
[Eliminated all 124 enemies]
Contribution:
Hudson Mitchell: 60%
Rebecca Harris: 22%
Anna Harris: 10%
Shawn Adams: 8%
Allocating rewards...
Congratulations! A certain god wants to be your new
potential patron.
2 skills levelled up.

Skill unlocked: Chaotic Battle Instinct.
The warrior taps into a primal, chaotic state of mind,
where reason and fear are overwhelmed by a flood of
instinctual combat prowess. While in this frenzied state,
the warrior's tactical acumen sharpens unpredictably,
allowing them to anticipate enemy movements with
uncanny precision and react with brutal efficiency.
However, this comes at a cost,rational thought becomes
distorted, and the warrior's actions may become
increasingly erratic and unpredictable, making them a
double-edged sword on the battlefield. This skill
increases attack speed, critical strike chance, and
grants a chance to counter enemy tactics with
unorthodox manoeuvres.

Gained armour: Savage spaulders

some spiky shoulder pads made of dark metal or something. Covered in weird carvings that might mean something, but probably don't. Straps? Yeah, they're red. Padding? Sure. They give +3% Vitality and +4% Dexterity because... magic, I guess. Legend says baby Deimos gnawed on these during a tantrum, then threw them at a goat. Now they're legendary. Great if you like not dying and looking kinda cool.

The description is still a bit shitty, but a win is a win. I then checked my status for progress.

Name: Hudson Mitchell
Rank: Mortal (F)
Class: Light Warrior
Patron #1: N/A
Patron #2: N/A
Patron #3: N/A

Skills:

- **Identify Level 1 [A]**
- **Low Pain Resistance Level 8 [P]**
- **Predatorial Vision Level 4 [A]**
- **Chaotic Battle Instinct Level 1 [A]**

Chapter 10. "When we see men of a contrary character, we should turn inwards and examine ourselves." , Confucius.

The battle was over. The blood had dried, the screams had faded, and the rewards were given. Yet, instead of examining the gifts before me, my mind was ensnared in a suffocating fog. Is this who I am now? A twisted reflection of the beast within, sacrificing my very soul for a fleeting moment of hollow triumph? Have I become something more monstrous than I ever feared? How foolish I've been. The thrill of battle, the intoxication of power, it blinded me, consumed me. I ignored everyone but myself. But what if I wasn't the only one? What if they too are harbouring secrets, playing their own games, with me as just another piece on their board? Am I the selfish one, or are we all just using each other, pretending to care until it no longer suits us? Is this truly who I'm meant to be?

I replayed the battle in my mind, recognizing my comrades, their faces blurred by my single-minded focus. But instead of feeling gratitude for their help, I merely acknowledged their positions, moving only where I could inflict the most damage. They were tools, pawns in a game that I had convinced myself was mine to win. But they're not.

Shawn, an admirable man, with a heart too big for this cruel world. Arrogant at times, but loyal to his people to a fault. As the eldest among us, he treated us like his children, as if it were his duty to shield us from the horrors we faced. His combat style reflected this: a natural tank, a soldier whose instincts were to protect rather than to destroy. He was a better man than I, for I could never be like him. I couldn't even fathom the strength it took to care that deeply, to fight with such selflessness.

Next was Rebecca, a true enigma. A predator by nature, her eyes always calculating, always assessing. A natural huntress, she chose her prey with care, avoiding battles she couldn't win. I thought we were alike, both prideful, both prioritising our own paths above all else. But I was wrong. She loved someone more than herself, her sister, Anna. A love so pure it was almost alien to me, something I couldn't grasp, let alone feel.

And Anna… even more of an enigma than Rebecca. A healer, yes, but not the fragile, innocent girl I had once believed her to be. When we started this journey, she was kinder than anyone, her heart bleeding for every drop of bloodshed. But this tutorial changed her, much like it changed us all. Or perhaps, like me, the tutorial only unearthed a side of her she never knew existed, a darkness lurking beneath the surface.

She blessed me despite never showing that ability before. Maybe she wasn't as naive as we thought, but instead portrayed herself that way out of convenience. As Stephen King once said, "The trust of the innocent is the liar's most useful tool." How true those words ring now.

And then there's me. An utterly contemptible excuse for a human being. I could blame my upbringing, the twisted childhood that shaped me, or the unfortunate circumstances I was thrust into, but none of that excuses the monster I've become. I only care for myself. I revel in the chaos, in the destruction, yet I despise myself for the suffering I cause. My paradoxical nature is not something I enjoy; it's just who I am. A walking contradiction, forever teetering on the edge between good and evil. Do I even have a conscience? Or is it merely the echo of a dying soul, desperately clinging to the remnants of its humanity?

This world we're trapped in seems to bring out the truth in people. The raw, unfiltered truth that we keep hidden even from ourselves. The Oracle told me Shawn wasn't the one to look out for, yet he's the most reliable. How ironic. I should have heeded the latter half of the Oracle's warning: "Trust no one." Maybe then I would have learned not to trust myself. Maybe then I would have seen the abyss lurking within me, waiting to consume me whole.

This nature of mine, it's a curse, a double-edged sword that cuts both ways. I fear it, but I also fear that the others see it too, that they're just waiting for the moment when I become more of a liability than an asset. Will they stand by me, or will they turn against me when the time comes? It's a double-edged sword, and I've been careless with how I wield it. How can I continue my path without addressing this? One wrong move, one moment of weakness, and it will lead to my demise. I need to understand who I am. I need to understand what drives me, what fuels the darkness inside me. Only then can I let go of my past and continue without regret. But for now, our priority is the tutorial.

Mission: Survive.
Time Limit: 17:21:38:24.
Survivors: 218/1000.

We still had more than half the time remaining, yet here I was, drowning in my own thoughts, paralyzed by introspection. How pathetic can I be? While others fight for survival, I'm lost in a mire of self-loathing and doubt. When I speak with my patron, I'll ask who I am, but will I even recognize the answer? Do I really want to know what lurks beneath this façade, or am I afraid that the truth will only confirm my worst fears, that I'm nothing more than the beast I've become?

Rebecca broke the sombre silence. "Alright, guys, we now know this truth. We can only trust ourselves." Her words were cold, calculated, a stark contrast to the warmth she once displayed.

Shawn was the first to respond. "Yeah, you're right. This was shit frankly. But we got to move on. After all, it might happen again." His voice was steady, reassuring, but there was an edge to it, a weariness that hadn't been there before. Even he was beginning to crack under the pressure.

Noticing the indifferent glare in Anna's eyes, I knew I had to shake myself out of my stupor. "Look, let's be honest with each other for once. We don't know each other. We pretend to, we trust each other in combat, but we don't truly know one another." I wasn't sure if I was convincing them or myself at this point. The words felt hollow, like a script I was reciting to keep the darkness at bay. "But the fact is, we need to move on. Things will only get tougher from here. I know for a fact that this battle caught the attention of some gods, so let's continue our struggles. I don't want to die, I've done too much to give up now. So please, let's move on." The plea in my voice was unmistakable, a desperation I could no longer hide.

With a few nods of agreement, we started moving toward a new destination. And at that moment it struck me. The real reason I didn't want to die was simple: it seemed like the coward's way out. A final escape from the torment that plagued me, the torment that I deserved. I will live if I want to; I will die if I have to. This is the only way I can make peace with the monster I've become. And hopefully, when this tutorial is dead and done, I will finally know who I am. Or perhaps, I will discover that there's nothing left to know.

We gathered around the hearth once again, the crackling flames doing little to break the sombre silence that enveloped us. Our relationships were more than just strained at this point; they were fraying at the edges. We relied on each other for survival, and that was about it. Yet, despite the tension, we had no choice but to continue down this path, so we had no choice but to begin to think of our next move.

"We can't just sit here," Shawn finally spoke up, his voice cracking under the weight of the nervous atmosphere. I could feel the others' eyes turn to him, their glares heavy with doubt. "We need a plan. Something that will allow us to move on. Please, does anyone have any ideas?"

He was right. A bit blunt, but correct nevertheless. He was still him, just more pragmatic. I couldn't tell if his intention was to motivate us or to expose his vulnerability, but either way, his words struck a chord. Before I could process what he'd said, Rebecca spoke up, her voice carrying a mix of fear and defiance.

"I need to confess something," she began, glancing around at us with a look that was equal parts fear and hostility. "In the last battle, I gained something… valuable, or at least I think it is. We've been fighting for our survival, and I just can't take it anymore. An interested goddess offered me an invitation to her sister's labyrinth. She said that it would be an intellectual challenge rather than physical. And I think that's what we need.."

There was defiance in her voice, almost as if she was issuing an ultimatum rather than making a suggestion. Join her, or lose her. I had countless questions, but it was clear she wasn't going to answer any of them.

"Okay, I think I agree with you. We all deserve a break," I said, masking my true thoughts. It wasn't physical exhaustion that plagued me, it was my mind that was unravelling. I needed to stop killing, to stop this endless cycle of violence, even if just for a moment. An intellectual journey might be exactly what I needed.

Shawn, however, wasn't ready to let it go. "Wait a second, are we not going to address the goddess-sized elephant in the room?" His voice was tense, the unspoken suspicion hanging between us. I could tell he was more comfortable around me than the twins, and his frustration was palpable.

"What's the problem, Shawn?" Anna snapped defensively. "My sister suggested something we all clearly need; a break! Why are you still so skeptical of us? Don't you think we've been through enough?"

"All I want to know is which goddess' labyrinth we're heading into," Shawn countered, his tone sharp despite his attempt to be polite. The message was clear: Don't try to take control without including us.

"I don't know!" Rebecca's voice rose in frustration. "All I know is that she's an Olympian goddess, close to the one who gave me the invitation. And no, I'm not going to tell you which goddess gave it to me because it's not important!" Her words dripped with hostility, making Shawn and I instinctively reach for our weapons before we realised we weren't in a battle.

Shawn hesitated, clearly torn between wanting to confront the issue and lacking the patience or respect to do so. He looked at me, almost pleading for support.

"Shawn, it's an Olympian. One of the twelve most powerful gods in the Greco-Roman pantheon. This is too big an opportunity to pass up," I said, my voice steady. I needed him to agree with me. I needed this break as much as anyone. After a moment of tension, he nodded, and I felt a wave of relief.

Anna spoke up next. "Alright, tomorrow we accept the invitation, and then we'll be teleported to the labyrinth." I clenched my fists, feeling a wave of disgust. How dare they share this information with each other and then spring it on us after they'd already made their decision? What else were they hiding?

Later that night, Shawn and I lay beside each other, the weight of the day pressing down on us. I spent my time reading the book, opening a random page and landing on the chapter on the history of Athens. But I was still uneasy, and sensing it, Shawn broke the silence.

"Today was fucked, man. We just finished a war, and not four hours later we're apparently chosen by an Olympian goddess. What kind of luck is that? I'm exhausted, but this is too big an opportunity to ignore. But I don't get it,why are the twins so against us? Don't you think what we've been through should have earned some trust by now? They aren't even grateful that without us, they'd be dead." he stated, clearly needing to get some stuff off his chest. Without allowing me to interrupt he continued on in an act of defense, " But at least we're getting a break, right? Not sure how much of a break it'll be, but it's something. Speaking of the labyrinth, who do you think it belongs to? And who do you think is Rebecca's 'secret little goddess'?"

I turned to face him, seeing the mischievous grin on his face. I couldn't help but laugh, appreciating his attempt to lighten the mood. "Alright, Shawn, use your brain for once-"

"Hey-" Shawn interrupted.

"Just listen, fatass," I teased, the lighthearted insult easing the tension. "Think about it. We're dealing with Olympian goddesses. The council usually includes Hera, Aphrodite, Demeter, Hestia, Artemis, and Athena. Out of all of them, it's pretty obvious whose labyrinth we're headed into."

I paused, letting the thought linger in the air. Shawn shifted beside me, clearly trying to piece it all together. I could see the gears turning in his head, but I wasn't going to hand him the conclusion. Part of me wanted him to work through it, to see if he'd come to the same realisation I had. But I couldn't help the small grin that crept onto my face, I already knew where this was going.

"If you think about it," I continued, keeping my voice measured, "Hestia's role has always been about stability, keeping the hearth burning, maintaining peace within the home. But does that really fit with the kind of challenge we're about to face? A labyrinth? That's not her style. It's about strategy, intellect… and who better embodies that than Athena?"

I glanced at Shawn, who looked like he was on the verge of asking more questions, but I didn't let him interrupt. "Then there's Athena's connection to Artemis. The two have always been close, both goddesses who value discipline, skill, and wisdom. And if you think about Rebecca's skills with the bow… Well, it makes sense, doesn't it?"

I let the implication hang. Shawn didn't need to know every detail swirling in my head. He just needed to know enough to trust the path we were on. And honestly, I wasn't entirely sure I wanted to voice my full thoughts out loud,there was something unsettling about the connections I was making.

"Anyway," I said, leaning back and letting the tension ease out of my voice, "it's just a theory. Could be Athena, could be Hestia. But given what we've seen, I'd say we're walking into Athena's domain. But who knows? Maybe we'll find out soon enough." I said whilst glancing at the chapter I was reading. It felt fitting that we would go into Athena's labyrinth when I was reading about her city.

Shawn groaned in frustration, but I could see the acceptance settling in his eyes. He didn't have to agree with me entirely, just enough to follow through. That was enough for now. I wasn't ready to lay all my cards on the table, especially not when the stakes were this high.

The next morning, we followed Rebecca, and with her nod, the world around us blurred, and the forest dissolved into a swirl of light and shadow. My stomach lurched as we were pulled through space, but the sensation quickly passed. When the world settled again, we stood on rough, uneven ground, the air cooler and scented with ancient stone and moss.

I blinked, adjusting to the dim light. Before us loomed the entrance to Athena's Labyrinth. The ruins surrounding it were both breathtaking and mournful,a haunting reminder of a forgotten past. The once-grand structure was now a mix of beauty and decay, its cracked columns wrapped in ivy, the worn carvings on the stone walls hinting at a glory long past.

Statues of owls, Athena's sacred creatures, flanked the entrance, their chipped eyes still commanding respect despite the ravages of time. The archway, a blend of majesty and ruin, stood firm, as if determined to protect whatever lay within.

Instinctively, I activated my Identify skill. The words appeared in my vision:

Athena's Labyrinth: Property of the Goddess of Wisdom. A trial for the mind, heart, and soul.

I shared the information with the others, my voice hushed by the weight of what lay before us. "This isn't just any labyrinth. It's Athena's, her trial."

Rebecca glanced at the worn carvings, a mix of awe and apprehension in her eyes. "So, this is it… the real test."

Anna nodded silently, gripping her staff tighter. Shawn let out a slow breath, his eyes tracing the crumbling ruins. "Whatever we face there, it's not just about fighting. We'll need more than brute strength."

I nodded, my gaze fixed on the dark, gaping maw of the labyrinth before us. The steps leading down were slick with moss, inviting us into the depths below. There was no turning back now. The labyrinth called to us, not just as a test of our abilities, but as a challenge to our very souls.

"We've come this far," I said, more to myself than to the others. "Let's see if we're worthy of what comes next."

And with that, I led the way, stepping forward into the shadows of Athena's Labyrinth, where beauty and ruin intertwined, and where our true trials were about to begin.

Chapter 12. "A prudent question is one-half of wisdom." , Francis Bacon.

As we entered the temple, we were greeted by a magnificent sight. The pillars, adorned in ivory, were engraved with masterful depictions of serpents and owls. Yet, these pillars were more than they appeared, upon closer inspection, they were intricately laced with bookshelves, their contents ever-changing, as if the knowledge within them was alive. The barren floor, stripped of the expected grandeur, seemed to reflect a deeper truth; a raw connection to the earth, perhaps mirroring the unsettled ground beneath our feet. With every step, the room seemed to pulse with disarray, the air thickened, the shadows deepened, as though chaos itself lived in these walls. The floor was strewn with unopened, yet clearly disturbed, boxes, as if someone had been searching for a specific one without caring for the contents of the others. Finally, my eyes landed on a solitary figure seated on a throne.

The man was both menacing and endearing, his demeanour a paradox of excitement and calm. I couldn't quite decipher his expression. One hand rested on a box, identical to those scattered around the floor. His throne was simple, with the only distinguishing feature being a serpent bust carved into the armrests. He looked at us with a complex gaze, a blend of sorrow, longing, and the faintest trace of gratitude; as if our presence was a bittersweet reminder of something lost. Then he spoke.

"Welcome, all, to my patron's labyrinth." His voice carried a weight of years hidden behind a youthful visage. "My patron brought you here at the request of her most trusted Olympian. She asked me to guide you, but first, I must judge whether you are worthy. If you can decipher who I am, I will grant you guidance. *Identify* will not work on me. However, in respect to my patron's wishes, I will allow each of you to ask one question, but you may not confer with each other."

We instantly recognized the power behind his words. I glanced at my companions, giving them silent permission to speak. This wasn't arrogance or pride, just the unsettling realisation that I might not have the answers they needed. Doubt gnawed at me, a familiar but unwelcome companion

Shawn, ever eager but often overlooked, spoke first. "Are you a former king of Athens who built a magnificent palace?" The moment he spoke, we all stared at him in disbelief. His question, though well-intentioned, left us all cringing in disbelief, stating something that was already obvious given the clues and the layout of the room.

The king gazed down at Shawn with a bemused smirk, clearly amused by his foolishness. "I'm genuinely astonished by your stupidity. Can you not read between the lines? Since this question is far more foolish than I anticipated, I'll give you a hint for your next question. Look around. This room is a window into my soul. It reflects what encompasses my entire being. This room is me… so, to answer your question, yes, I was a king in Athens." He shook his head, seemingly irritated by the need to state the obvious. I couldn't blame him, what king doesn't sit on a throne? Shawn had asked a foolish question, reducing our chances.

However, the hint the king provided was incredibly significant. When I first entered the room, I believed it to be a reflection of Athena, since this was her test. But certain things didn't add up. Why would Athena, known as the most organised Olympian, be represented by both order and chaos? If this were Hermes' temple, I would understand the clutter. But now I realised the clutter was part of this man's soul. He himself was in turmoil. But this wasn't enough for me. Why was the floor left bare, raw and unrefined? Why did the serpent dominate over the owl, as if one side of him struggled to overpower the other? And what was the significance of the boxes? These things puzzled me. I understood their presence but not their importance to the man before me.

Rebecca spoke next. "What's with the boxes?" Her voice, sharp with frustration, carried more than just anger; there was a deep-seated urgency, as if she was defending something far more personal, which made sense given that Shawn's absurd question had cast doubt on our group. I could hear the frustration in her voice. As she asked the question, she glared at Shawn. In her glare, I caught a flicker of something darker, a wound that had been festering long before this encounter, something that had grown more intense since the incident.

The king responded after a moment's hesitation, likely due to the disrespectful tone of her question. "Hmm, while I dislike the way you asked, I shall forgive you, given that tensions are clearly running high. To answer your question, the boxes are crucial to my upbringing. They are the reason I am who I am. I don't know why there are many of them here, but I do know that this box-" he pointed to the small box next to him, "-is the reason I am here."

This response provided more clues. I was slowly connecting the dots. A man deeply connected to boxes from a young age, a man who became king, a man beloved by Athena. But what was their relationship? Was it like that of mother and son? Lovers? I still wasn't sure. Why were the serpents more prominent than the owls in this room? Shouldn't a king give more respect to his patron? What if the serpents represented him, just like the boxes did? I was racking my brain, trying to recall myths involving serpents, boxes, and the goddess of wisdom.

While I was lost in thought, Anna spoke. "This may be a gamble, but were you raised under the guidance of the goddess of wisdom, and are you connected with the founding of Athens' most sacred traditions?" This was the question I needed, a calculated risk to probe the relationship between this man and the goddess of wisdom. But there was a greater risk in the fact that she had asked two questions in one. I feared his response. I still didn't have all the information I needed. I prayed he wouldn't lose his temper; too many times, I'd seen anger turn to violence, decisions made in haste that cost lives. This felt all too familiar. I knew the danger of trying to trick a superior.

His voice dropped, laced with a controlled fury. "You dare test me with trickery? Your insolence would have earned you severe consequences were it not for the rules that bind me. But you know what? I'll play along. I will answer both of your questions, but in return," he pointed directly at me, "Decipher who I am, and do so without aid. Alone, stripped of your allies' insights, can you stand against the weight of expectation, or will you fracture like all those before you?" My stomach tightened as his words sank in. I cursed silently, realising his true intention. He wanted to break us, to test not just our wits but our unity. He doubted my intelligence, clearly. He wanted to make it clear that he didn't care about what I had to say. He wanted to sow discord within our group. After all, he was not yet our guide.

"Lady Athena did indeed raise me, something for which I am forever grateful. And yes, she entrusted me with the responsibility of founding Athens' most sacred traditions. So, do you think you know who I am?"

My mind raced, but for the first time, clarity began to emerge from the chaos. I could feel the pieces aligning, a strange confidence building as I connected the dots. The boxes symbolise his birth. He was raised by Athena. Serpents were linked to his myth. He was one of the most important kings in Athens' history. I had to piece it together. Wait, I read about him before. Just the night before in fact. It felt too convenient to be simply a coincidence. So with a deep breath I began relaying my thoughts.

"You are the earth-born king of Athens, nurtured by Athena, founder of sacred traditions, and a symbol of divine wisdom,Erichthonius."

The king smiled at me with a newfound respect, his gaze wandering as if inviting me to elaborate on the reasoning behind my deduction before he would fully accept it. I took a deep breath, gathering my thoughts before speaking. "You presented us with a riddle wrapped in this room, a reflection of your soul, as you said. The moment we stepped inside, the pillars adorned with both serpents and owls caught my attention. The serpents, far more prominent, hinted at something beyond Athena's usual symbolism. It was clear that the serpents were not just decorations, they represented a deep connection to your very being.

The floor, left bare and earthy, spoke of a connection to the earth itself, a clue that led me to consider someone born of the earth, as you were. The cluttered state of the room, with unopened boxes scattered about, suggested turmoil, a lingering connection to the very circumstances of your birth. The fact that the boxes are central to your identity, as you yourself mentioned, pointed me directly to the myth of the infant hidden in a chest, a symbol of your early life under Athena's care.

When you confirmed that you were raised by Athena and tasked with establishing sacred traditions in Athens, the pieces fell into place. Only one figure in Athenian legend is so closely tied to both Athena and serpents, who was earth-born and played such a pivotal role in the city's early history.

You are Erichthonius, the earth-born king of Athens, nurtured by Athena herself. The serpents reflect your unique birth and identity, the boxes of your early life, and the traditions you founded at the very core of Athens' culture. All these clues converge to reveal your true identity."

The king's stern expression softened, just slightly, as if reluctantly impressed. "Not bad," he conceded, amusement barely masking a newfound respect. "You are better than I expected. You are indeed correct, and I will guide you through this labyrinth.

Firstly, I will explain what this labyrinth entails. The labyrinth is no mere trial; it is a reflection of your fears, your doubts, your resolve. Each floor will strip away your assumptions, test not just your wits but the very fabric of your bond. The first floor will confront your wits and strength, two forces often at odds... but the strength you need isn't what you think

The second floor is a test of the body. You will face a trial where your individual strengths mean nothing unless bound by trust. Alone, you will falter. Together, you might stand a chance.

The third floor is where most falter. A test of the eyes. It would ruin the surprise to tell you more.

The fourth floor is a battle of the souls. Simple, right? Just the strongest foe you have ever faced.

The fifth floor is pure combat. Simple as that. I wonder how you will face this.

And on that happy note, it is time to begin. I will give you ten minutes to speak, to prepare, though nothing can truly prepare you for what lies ahead. Use your time wisely, for once you begin, there will be no turning back, and no second chances. The labyrinth sees all, and it does not forgive."

Chapter 13. " The more man plans, The more God laughs." , Yiddish Proverb.

We sat on the barren earth beneath the oppressive gaze of the powerful king. It was clear his role went beyond mere guidance. His eyes pierced through us, probing our thoughts. Time ticked by, his true intent unmistakable. He didn't want us to plan, nor to prosper. He wanted to test us. Yet, one of us seemed oblivious to his scrutiny.

"Alright then, any plans on how we're going to do this?" Shawn, with his usual knack for breaking tension, spoke up. His ignorance was a gift I hadn't realised I needed. Without him, the precious minutes we had to plan would have slipped away unnoticed.

Anna followed suit, her voice laced with unease. "I don't even know how we're supposed to plan this. We can't plan for what we don't know." Her voice betrayed the panic she tried to suppress. Too many things were still unknown.

Rebecca's voice sliced through the air, low and venomous, like a predator ready to strike. "If we have to hunt something, leave it to me." she said, her tone dripping with arrogance. "None of you will be much help. What happens to the beast is my decision, and I won't discuss it. Don't you remember, Hudson? That first day? Your arrogance got us all hurt. What if something had happened to my sister? I'm done following your lead, only to worry more about her afterward. You know I'm right."

Her words hit like poison-tipped daggers. She wanted me to feel the sting. It was a shocking turn. But I suppose that meant Shawn was right. Her sympathy is unnecessary. I had done too much for her, fought a Chimera for her. How dare she question me? She wanted to surpass me, but I wouldn't allow it. Not now. Not ever.

"Shut the fuck up, Harris."

"What did you say?"

"Enough about your sister!" I snapped, my voice laced with venom. "You think she's the only one that matters? There are four of us here, not just her!"

Rebecca's glare was ice cold, her eyes burning with fury. "If you weren't so arrogant, maybe we wouldn't have been hurt in the first place! What if she had died, Hudson? What then?"

"Arrogant?" I laughed, the sound hollow. "We fought a fucking Chimera to save you! What more do you want from us, Rebecca? You think your suffering is the only one that matters? We've all bled, we've all lost, but you don't give a damn!"

"I don't need you, Hudson. I don't need anyone. Just stay out of my way." Her words were deliberate, too sharp to be casual. She wanted me to react, to lose my cool. But why? Was she trying to provoke me, or was she testing how far I'd go?

"Shut the fuck up!" My voice boomed, louder than I intended. The others flinched. "I'm sick of your bullshit authority. You're not the only one in this game. We survive together, or none of us make it out alive. Get that through your head."

Rebecca's lips curled into a sneer. "I don't trust you. Not anymore."

"I don't care." My words dripped with bitterness. "We hunt the beast. We work together. End of story."

Beep!
An enraged goddess openly shows hostility.
A potential patron is proud of your defiance.

I felt the weight of my rage lift, but I didn't care about the consequences. As the tension melted from my shoulders, I looked around at the reactions of my companions.

Shawn's face was frozen in shock, his eyes wide at my outburst. His brows furrowed in confusion, almost as if asking why I spoke now. Shawn's smile was faint, too controlled. He agreed with me, but he was holding something back. Was it fear? Or was he just relieved I said what he couldn't?

Anna was expressionless, her eyes hollow and lifeless. She looked at me like a statue, her gaze a deep, unreadable abyss. Her face betrayed nothing, but I sensed an undercurrent of hatred hidden beneath the surface.

Ericthonius was the most surprising. His devilish grin spread wide as he glanced between Rebecca and me. He wasn't allowed to interfere, as per his promise, but his excitement was palpable. His eyes flickered with amusement as he calculated all the possibilities. He was supposed to guide us, but I couldn't tell if his help would lead to salvation or ruin.

But it was Shawn who defused the situation with a heavy sigh. "Let's not focus on it. Planning for an ethical dilemma before we even know what it is won't help us."

Anna spoke next, her voice devoid of emotion. "I think there are only two floors where we'll need to work together. The others will test individual intelligence. We need to figure out the fifth-floor boss and solve the riddle on the first floor together. But after that, there's no need to stay together. Frankly, I think we need some time apart. Tensions are too high."

Her words carried reason, each one carefully selected. It felt like Anna was stepping out of the shadows for the first time. She'd always been quiet, lurking on the edges of our plans, but now... now she was speaking up, guiding us. Why now? Anna wasn't the harmless healer we thought she was. A healer is supposed to be the most trustworthy, the one who keeps us alive when everything falls apart. The peaceful, the kind. But now I wasn't so sure. The healer, after all, decides who lives... and who doesn't.

That day, I learned never to underestimate a healer.

Chapter 14. "Dare to know! Have the courage to use your own understanding" , Immanuel Kant.

Cold. That was the only way I could begin to describe the atmosphere. I was angry at Rebecca, maybe at myself? But honestly, I couldn't care less about that. I said what I wanted to say. It doesn't matter what my reputation is now. Why should I care about others' opinions of me? This whole time, I've been tiptoeing around these people since the moment I arrived. But no more. They may not have forced me into this situation, but they sure as hell had a hand in shaping my new outlook on life.

A loud clap snapped me out of my rage. "Hahaha, who would've thought?" Ericthonius was clearly enjoying our disagreement. "The group of four is actually two groups of two. This is enlightening."

"When are we starting this damn test?" Was I being disrespectful? Perhaps. Did I care? Not at all.

The king looked down at me, and for a brief moment, I could feel my skin prickle with a flash of bloodlust. "Patience, Hudson. Your trial will begin soon enough. But know this: even if you conquer the challenge ahead, not all of you will leave this labyrinth."

"What the hell!" Rebecca spat through gritted teeth, fury radiating from her. "This wasn't the deal! I came here for an intellectual challenge, not a death sentence. My patron promised safety, protection, she wouldn't let us die. You're telling me now one of us won't leave? What the actual fuck? My patron told me it would be safe!"

The king froze for what felt like an eternity, time itself seeming to halt. Then slowly, the corners of his mouth lifted into a cruel smile, and his laughter boomed. "You mortals are so predictable. Do you truly believe you command the unwavering attention of an Olympian? You are but a fleeting amusement. A mortal, one of many. You are no favoured child of the gods. She has yet to claim you. So do not presume to speak as if her gaze belongs only to you."

Life drained from Rebecca's eyes as if she were pleading for him to say it was a joke. But the king's demeanour never faltered; he was the very image of authority. However, I was preoccupied with other thoughts. The king's words left little to the imagination. An Olympian, with maidens who serve her, huntresses in her wake. The disdain for mortal arrogance... it pointed to one goddess: Artemis. Patron of the hunt, protector of her own. But Artemis doesn't favour just anyone. Her attention is fierce, protective only to those she claims. The thought lingered in my mind; could Artemis be the goddess angered with me as well? But that led to a more critical question: which deity stood in my corner?

"Can you explain how the first floor works?" I had never been more thankful for Shawn's presence. He always knew the right thing to say, whether he meant to or not. Right now, he was the only one I trusted.

"Fine," the king replied, his voice void of any emotion. "You will each be separated and given a riddle with a one-word answer. You will then be transported back here, where you will solve the final puzzle. If you're correct, you pass. The punishment for failure will be at my discretion." His tone carried an air of authority and amusement, as if we were merely toys for his entertainment. Any respect we might have earned was now gone. He wanted us to know our place, and we got the message loud and clear. "Now, without further ado, let's begin."

The moment the king clapped, I was transported to a small room with a single desk. The air pressed down on me, thick and suffocating, as though it sought to smother any hope of escape. Every breath tasted stale, like the scent of decay had permeated the very walls. Cold sweat trickled down my spine, each drop a reminder of the growing dread.. A note appeared in my mind: "This room was plucked from your memory. We can't make things too easy, can we?" An intense hatred coursed through me. The king knew exactly what he was doing, why this room was one I loathed. It would have been easier if I felt only anger. But I didn't. Fear gripped me like icy fingers tightening around my throat, each heartbeat reverberating in my ears as if the room itself was amplifying my terror.

Fear. The word feels too small, too insignificant for what clawed at my insides. This wasn't just fear, it was true terror that twisted my gut, a predator lurking in the darkness, waiting to pounce the moment I let my guard down. People toss it around casually, but they don't know what real fear is. Real fear constricts your very being, drives daggers into your heart. It's not just a reaction; it's a formidable and dangerous enemy, one that takes true willpower to overcome. Fear burrowed deep, threading itself through every thought, every breath, like a parasite feeding on your sanity, waiting for the moment when you think you're safe, only to rear its head again. Fear isn't scary, it's fatal. And that was the emotion coursing through me in this room. How could I forget? This was the room where I learned to trust only myself, the room that awakened my instincts. But I didn't want to think about it. This room had a tragic past, and it was blocking me from the task at hand.

I moved toward the centre of the room. Its murky, pungent smell wrapped around my soul like a noose. How unsettling that they could even replicate that. At the centre of the room lay a tattered old cloth with a handwritten riddle:

"I work with precision, my craft is unique.
My tools are my limbs, though not what you'd think.
My handiwork glistens, though it's often unseen,
But if you get too close, you'll be caught in between."

As I read the riddle, my heart pounded faster, not just because of the challenge but because this dark, suffocating space was closing in on me. The silence was deafening, broken only by the thud of my pulse pounding in my ears. Every creak in the walls felt like the building itself was breathing, waiting, watching, for me to break. The flickering light cast monstrous, twisting shadows that seemed alive, reaching out from the walls as if mocking my vulnerability. I could almost hear whispers from those dark corners, taunting me with the inevitability of my fate.. I forced myself to focus on the words, fighting the weight of the past pressing down on me.

"I work with precision, my craft is unique." I repeated the words aloud, convincing myself that I was allowed to speak. I was never allowed to speak in this place, not really. I picture ancient artisans, Daedalus, who crafted wings to escape, or the master weavers of old. Their hands, their skills, each movement deliberate. But something about this doesn't sit right. No, this isn't about a person. The word "limbs" in the next line pulls me toward something more… unsettling. **"My tools are my limbs, though not what you'd think."** Limbs as tools. Animals, perhaps? A creature. My thoughts wander to the serpents in the underworld, slithering and binding all they touch, but they don't build, they destroy. This creature is a maker, a weaver. It uses its body in ways unexpected.

I glance at the shadows again. My chest tightens. This room feels like a trap itself, a reminder of that night I never speak of; the night I was cornered, helpless. I need to focus on the riddle. I need to solve it to escape this suffocating place.

"My handiwork glistens, though it's often unseen." My breath catches in my throat. Glistens? Something delicate, something hidden in the dark, almost invisible. I can't shake the feeling that this clue is leading me somewhere I don't want to go, somewhere familiar but filled with dread. A spider perhaps? Athena's hatred of the spider is well known. A spider, the way it weaves its traps, glistening in the darkness, waiting for prey. Why? Why can I not bring myself to think of other possibilities?

Part of me doesn't want this to be the answer. Part of me remembers the spider, remembers the helpless feeling of being caught in a web I couldn't escape. Not a literal web, no, but it might as well have been. The trauma feels just as sticky, just as constraining. I need to breathe.

If I solve this, I get out. If I don't… Well, I can't think about that.

For a moment, I wonder if I'm jumping to conclusions too quickly. I consider other possibilities, desperately wanting to avoid the one I know is lurking. Could it be Hephaestus, the crippled god who forged intricate mechanisms, his handiwork often unseen until it sprang into action? Or perhaps an ant lion, with its pit of sand, hidden until its prey stumbles in? But neither of these quite fit. Hephaestus doesn't work with limbs in this way. And ant lions, they're too small, too literal. This feels grander, more mythological. The craft, the weaving, it keeps pulling me back to the idea of a web.

And then, the final line: **"If you get too close, you'll be caught in between."** My heart skips. The web. It's always the web. That's how it felt the night everything collapsed. I couldn't move, couldn't escape the grip of fear, of everything unravelling around me. Just like a web, unseen until you're already caught in its sticky threads. I don't want to admit it, but I know the answer now. The spider.

I hate this answer. It brings up too many memories, too many emotions I've tried so hard to bury. But I can't stay in this room, in this dark, oppressive place. The walls feel like they're pressing in on me, the shadows moving closer, almost breathing. I think of insects that normally would never cross my mind. Is this how they felt when caught in a spider's web? They must have felt this way when they realised their fate,

I need to solve this and get out.

The answer is spider. It has to be. Everything fits,the precision, the hidden handiwork, the trap. Athena's hatred. I whisper the word, feeling both relief and fear as it passes my lips. "Spider." The room seems to shudder for a moment, as if acknowledging my answer. I hear a small chime and I am once again teleported to the room which is governed under the eyes of an oppressive king.

Chapter 15. "Stubbornness destroys good advice." ,- Ali ibn Abi Talib

Rebecca's POV:

After solving the riddle, we all stumbled back into the room under the ever-watchful eye of that absolutely god-awful king. His presence loomed over us like a shadow. The tricks he played were cruel and relentless, his entire demeanour oozing superiority. What the hell is his problem? He calls himself our guide, yet pulls us into the deepest, most traumatic recesses of our minds. To think I had to stand in that cursed house again... He better have known that memory wouldn't destroy me. No way I'd let it.

If it were up to me, that place would've burned to ash long ago.

I glanced around at the others. My sister, my only family in this hellhole, stood there, trying to mask her fear. Her attempt at composure might have fooled the others, but not me. I could see the tension in her shoulders, the distant look in her eyes. She was trying so hard to be the unshakable force I knew she wanted to be, but the past had a way of digging its claws into you when you least expected it. Still, I admired her strength. My sister had always been a rock in our family, even when everything was falling apart. But here? In this place? That look on her face told me everything I needed to know. She was barely hanging on.

Then there was Shawn, grinning like a fool. Of all things, smiling. I couldn't wrap my head around it. After what we just experienced? After being dragged through our worst memories? He had the nerve to smile? I knew his memory must have been just as torturous, if not worse, and yet, here he was, with that smug grin plastered on his face. What kind of twisted idiot grins after such torment? I clenched my fists, silently fuming. The minute he screws up, the moment he lets any of us down, I'll be the one to put an arrow between his shoulder blades. That much I'm sure of.

And then, there was Hudson, an absolute wreck. Sweat dripped down his face, his hands trembling slightly. I could almost smell the fear rolling off him in waves. I watched as he desperately tried to control his breathing, to compose himself. His eyes were wide and frantic, but I could see him forcing the light back into them, fighting to stay in control. At least he wasn't entirely useless. The longer I watched, the more he seemed to regain his composure, bit by bit. But just as I thought he was pulling himself together, I felt it, a flash of something dark. Pure, unfiltered bloodlust radiated from him. It was so quick, so subtle, but I felt it hit me like a punch to the gut.

For a split second, Hudson wasn't just a scared man; he was a monster.

It was almost ironic. The so-called "monster" was the first to speak. His voice, though still shaky, broke the tension in the room. "Spider. That's what I got."

My sister was next. "Competition," she said quietly, her voice barely above a whisper. She was still trying to push through her trauma. I could hear it in the tremor of her words.

Then came the idiot, Shawn. "Weaving," he announced, as if this whole thing was some kind of joke.

I crossed my arms and smiled, feeling the familiar surge of pride swell within me. Of course, I had the most challenging riddle, the toughest answer. "Blasphemy," I declared confidently, my eyes daring them to question me.

They all looked at me, wide-eyed. Naturally. They knew I always had the hardest tasks, the most difficult challenges, and yet I came out on top every time.

"Obviously, this is a famous battle," I said, breaking the silence. "A blasphemous one. A battle against the gods." I turned to Hudson, my voice dripping with condescension. "Hudson, make yourself useful for once and tell me about the battles where mortals dared defy the divine."

Hudson nodded, still trying to pull himself together. It was almost pathetic, the way he jumped to fulfil my command. "There are several battles," he began, "across different mythologies: Greek, Egyptian, African. But since this is Athena's temple, it's most likely Greek."

I couldn't help but scoff. Greek? How predictable. "Greek?" I repeated, rolling my eyes. "This is Athena's labyrinth, the goddess of wisdom. She wouldn't make it that simple." I put extra emphasis on the word *wisdom*, just to hammer in how clueless he truly was.

Hudson's temper flared slightly, his frustration beginning to show. "What are you even talking about, Rebecca? This *is* a Greek labyrinth, dedicated to a Greek goddess. There's no way it's anything else. It wouldn't make sense!"

"Hudson. I almost feel sorry for you," I replied coldly, my words sharp as knives. I could tell I wasn't getting through to him. I glanced at my sister again, still too shaken to be of any help, and then at Shawn, who was watching our exchange like it was some sort of sport. Useless, both of them. Once again, it fell to me, the only capable one here, to save this group from inevitable failure

Hudson, however, wasn't finished. His voice rose, frustration bubbling to the surface. "How stupid are you? Why won't you even listen? Don't you think I have a reason for saying it's the battle between Arachne and Athena, and not something like Anansi versus Nyame? It's *obvious*! It fits with everything we've seen here! The Chimaera, the Greek influences, this is clearly Greek!"

I smirked, watching as Hudson unknowingly played right into my hands. I had him exactly where I wanted him. "The answer is Anansi versus Nyame," I declared triumphantly.

The king immediately clapped his hands, signalling that my answer had been locked in. It was done. Victory was mine. But I couldn't shake the feeling of tension that still hung heavy in the air. Something was wrong.

Hudson's POV:

What. The. Hell.

I had no other words to describe what had just happened. She hadn't even *tried* to listen to me. It was beyond frustrating. I stared at Rebecca, my mind racing, struggling to comprehend how someone could be so... *dense*. So completely absorbed in her own arrogance that she couldn't see the truth right in front of her. The pieces fit. Everything pointed to Arachne and Athena. How could she be so blind?

Before I could speak, the king's voice echoed through the room, cutting through my thoughts like a knife. "Pathetic. That is what you are, Rebecca Harris. You are incorrect. The system will allocate points, or take them, from you soon. But first, Hudson, I want to hear your thoughts."

Rebecca, as always, couldn't keep her mouth shut. "Wait, how am I wrong? That doesn't make any sense!" she snapped, clearly offended.

The king's eyes narrowed, and the weight of his authority filled the room. "Did I grant you permission to speak, mortal? Silence until I deem it otherwise.," The king's voice cut through the air like ice, his gaze sliding to Rebecca as though she were nothing more than a nuisance. His eyes lingered for a moment, cold and unforgiving, before shifting to Hudson. "Speak. Now."

I took a deep breath, knowing I had to make this count. "I could hardly believe what I was witnessing, Your Majesty. She wouldn't even *consider* my reasoning. It was infuriating, like talking to a wall." I began, still reeling from the situation. "It didn't matter that I laid out the facts clearly. She dismissed me without a second thought, blinded by her own arrogance. It was maddening, standing there, knowing I was right about Arachne and Athena and being completely ignored."

The king's gaze remained steady, his eyes a mixture of curiosity and disdain. "Why did you choose that battle?"

I straightened my posture, trying to focus. "The myth of Arachne goes like this: she boasted about her skill in weaving, claiming it surpassed even the goddess Athena's. Athena, enraged by the blasphemy, accepted the challenge. Arachne wove a tapestry that exposed the gods' cruelty, while Athena's tapestry depicted their kindness. According to some versions, the result was a draw. But Athena, unable to tolerate such disrespect, punished Arachne by turning her into a spider. Arachne would weave forever, as a symbol of her arrogance. The words we were given, spider, competition, weaving, blasphemy,all fit this myth perfectly."

The king gave me a silent nod, urging me to continue.

"There's more," I added, gathering my thoughts. "It wasn't just a myth. This whole tutorial has been filled with Greek influences, the Chimera we fought, the architecture, even the atmosphere. Everything screams Greek mythology. It was too coincidental for the answer to be anything else. This was clearly meant to test our knowledge of Athena's domain."

the king's lips curled into the faintest shadow of a smile, an expression devoid of warmth. His eyes, however, remained as cold and calculating as ever. "You surprised me, Hudson. Few mortals possess the capacity to piece together such riddles; perhaps you are not entirely worthless." he said, his voice carrying a note of approval. "You are correct. But, as for the others... they must be punished."

Rebecca, of course, exploded in anger. "This is favouritism! Why should Hudson get rewarded while we suffer? This is completely unfair!"

The king didn't even flinch. In fact, his expression grew more amused. "Yes," he said, his voice dripping with condescension. "It *is* favouritism. And what are you going to do about it?"

Rebecca's face twisted in fury, but before she could retort, the king's voice turned cold again. "Rebecca. You have crossed the line once too often. Your punishment will be severe. I need not remind you, my mercy has limits."

A heavy silence fell over the room. I could feel the weight of the king's words as they hung in the air. I had expected him to be strict, but this... this was something else entirely. For the first time in a long while, I felt a shiver of fear run down my spine.

The king waved his hand dismissively, his patience clearly wearing thin. "Enough grumbling. You will all be teleported to your next trial soon. But remember this, any more disrespect, and your punishment will be severe."

Beep!
You have incorrectly guessed the riddle.
By the benevolence of the king, you are permitted to continue in this labyrinth.
One day has passed.
Congratulations! You were specifically chosen to be rewarded by the king's judgement.

I looked at my status window, the details flickering before me:

Name: Hudson Mitchell
Rank: Mortal (F)
Class: Light Warrior
Patron #1: N/A
Patron #2: N/A
Patron #3: N/A
Skills:

- **Identify Level 1 [A]**
- **Low Pain Resistance Level 8 [P]**
- **Predatorial Vision Level 7 [A]**
- **Chaotic Battle Instinct Level 3 [A]**

I don't really know what changed, but I felt it. My mind was more clear, more methodical. It felt as if I was more in tune with this world. There were many possibilities in moving forward. My path began to take shape.

But the moment was short-lived. From the corner of my eye, I saw Rebecca grumbling, clearly frustrated by her loss. She muttered something about losing levels, her pride wounded. For a moment, I felt a pang of pity for her. Then, something darker settled in.

Maybe, I thought, *it would be better if she didn't make it through this labyrinth.*

Wait. What? Did I just think that?

Since when have I become so indifferent about life and death? Since when did I start playing this game so loosely?

I wasn't like Rebecca. I wasn't... a monster was I?

The king's voice cut through my spiralling thoughts. "Enough," he said. "Your second trial awaits. Hunt the beast or perish. There will be no second chances."

Before we could react, the king waved his hand, and in an instant, we were whisked away once again, teleported to another world.

Chapter 16: "You have your way. I have my way. As for the right way, it does not exist." , Nietzsche

Some might say it's unfortunate that I still haven't grown accustomed to these sudden, unannounced transports to other realms. It's unnerving, I admit. One moment, I'm standing in one place, and the next, I'm hurtling through time and space, deposited somewhere foreign, with no warning or preparation. But unlike most, I don't consider it a misfortune. I've come to see these moments as a gift. Each time I regain consciousness, I am granted the opportunity to experience a childlike wonder, a wonder that makes the unknown feel less terrifying and more... magical.

This time, we found ourselves on a sun-kissed stretch of coast, the scent of salt and brine sharp in the air. The sun hung low in the sky, casting a golden glow over everything it touched. The gentle hiss of the waves played a constant rhythm as the tide ebbed and flowed, lapping at the shore with a slow, hypnotic cadence. It was almost as if the ocean itself were inviting us to relax, to forget why we were here. The sand beneath my feet was warm and velvety, moulding around each step, tempting me to lie down and surrender to the island's tranquil beauty.

But something about this peace felt deceptive. Beneath the calm, I could sense an undercurrent of tension, a hum of something more, something unseen, that belied the serenity of the island. I had learned long ago to trust my instincts in places like this. We might be in paradise, but paradise, I knew, could just as easily be a trap.

Despite this, the most captivating sight on the island was the lush, vibrant greenery of the trees that surrounded us. Each tree seemed to have a distinct personality, towering above us like gentle guardians, swaying in the ocean breeze. They stood tall, strong, as if they had weathered centuries of storms and remained untouched. The entire island, with its perfect landscape, seemed designed to soothe, to calm. From the soothing sounds of the waves to the gentle rustling of the leaves, everything about this place seemed to urge me to relax, to let go of the ever-present weight on my shoulders.

But I couldn't let go. Not here. Perhaps the island's allure was the very test the king had designed for us. Maybe this was part of the challenge, to see if we could resist the temptation of comfort and stay focused on our true mission.

As I was contemplating this, something caught my eye. Not far from where we stood, a stone pillar jutted out of the sand. It looked ancient, weathered by time, its surface rough and cracked. It seemed out of place in such a natural paradise. Its stark, concrete form was a harsh contrast to the island's organic beauty. We approached it cautiously, our weapons still sheathed but ready. As we drew nearer, I noticed inscriptions roughly carved into the surface.

"Look at this," Anna said softly, stepping forward. She was our healer, the one who always kept her head when the rest of us were ready to lose ours. She ran her fingers over the carvings, her brow furrowed. "It's a riddle," she said, her voice barely more than a whisper. And then she read aloud:

"In ocean's depths, a creature sleeps,
A beast that neither crawls nor leaps.
Half serpent's tail, half fish's might,
Its power is hidden from mortal sight.
Hunters seek it, far and wide,
To claim a prize that gods would hide.
For in its flesh, a secret lies,
The power to make Olympus die.
Now you must choose, a path to take,
Will you slay, or mercy make?
To end its life could break the sky,
But sparing it may leave gods to lie.
A hunter's choice, to still or free,
Which fate will rule your destiny?
Capture its form, or burn its heart,
Tell me, hunter, where do you start?"

Anna paused, letting the weight of the riddle sink in. She looked back at us, her usually calm demeanour showing the faintest flicker of frustration. "Why a riddle now? I thought there would be a change of pace," she said, her voice tinged with annoyance. It was rare to see Anna irritated, but it seemed even the king could test her patience.

"It is a moral dilemma," I pointed out, stepping closer to the pillar and running my eyes over the last lines. "Look at the final stanza."

Shawn, who had been trailing behind, looked utterly confused. "Uh… what's a stanza?" he asked, his voice full of genuine curiosity. Sometimes, it was hard not to smile at his innocence.

I sighed, but patiently. "A stanza is just a verse, Shawn. The last two lines give us a choice. We have to decide: do we kill the beast or capture it?"

I let the silence hang, waiting to see who would be the first to respond. The decision seemed obvious to me, but I didn't want to push the group. They needed to come to the conclusion themselves. No point in showing my hand too early.

Rebecca was the first to speak, and predictably, she wasn't subtle about it. "Why are we even wasting time talking about this? It'd be easier to kill the thing and be done with it. Even if it's just a baby, we're hunting it, which means it'll probably try to kill us, too. Let's just kill it and move on."

Her bluntness caught me off guard. I always thought her arrogance was just bluster, a mask she wore to hide something deeper. But in that moment, I realised there was a part of her that genuinely didn't care. But I was pissed off.

"The phrase 'make Olympus die' doesn't necessarily mean the gods themselves will fall," I said, my tone even and measured. "It could be a metaphor, a warning about something worse that might happen if we act recklessly."

I watched her closely as I spoke. This wasn't about showing mercy; it was about being strategic. And if I'm being completely honest, part of me just wanted to see her smug certainty crumble a little. I'm no noble hero, I have my petty moments like anyone else. Watching Rebecca falter would be a small victory.

She scoffed, rolling her eyes. "What beast could possibly take down Olympus? I've read that book you carry around like it's your lifeline. There's no creature powerful enough to do that. Typhon came close, but this? It's not that dangerous."

Before I could respond, Shawn spoke up, surprisingly defending me. "Hey, Rebecca, give him a chance. He's good with riddles, and he knows more mythology than any of us. Let's at least hear him out."

Shawn had an uncanny ability to diffuse tension. I was silently grateful for his intervention. It gave me time to think, to refocus on the riddle. The description of a creature that was neither serpent nor fish tugged at something deep in my memory. I started to sift through possibilities, legends and creatures that could match the description.

And then it hit me: the Ophiotaurus. A half-bull, half-serpent beast. The legends said that burning its entrails granted the power to overthrow the gods.

But what if I was wrong? I considered other possibilities: Charybdis, the sea monster known for creating whirlpools; the Hydra, whose regenerative heads made it almost impossible to kill. But none of them fit the prophecy of gods falling. The Kraken? No, too straightforward. The answer had to be something more elusive, something tied specifically to Olympus.

The more I thought about it, the more certain I became. The Ophiotaurus was the only creature that made sense. It was linked to Olympus' fate, and its heart was the key.

As I explained my reasoning to the others, a dangerous thought crept into my mind. If we killed it, could we truly gain the power of the gods? The temptation was undeniable, but I pushed it aside. That wasn't the kind of strength I wanted. Power without meaning, without sacrifice, it was hollow. I wasn't about to take that path.

Sensing the shift in the group's mood, Anna quickly changed the subject. "Let's focus on finding the creature first. We can deal with the moral dilemma later. Sis, you take point. You're the best hunter."

I watched as Rebecca's confidence swelled. Anna was feeding her ego, but why? Before I could dwell on it further, we gathered around the campfire at the centre of our camp. The hearth flickered, casting long shadows across the ground as we settled in for the night.

I sat down, my legs heavy from the day's journey. For the first time in what felt like years, I took a moment to gaze up at the night sky. The stars were brilliant, unpolluted by the haze of city lights, their sharp brilliance cutting through the darkness like diamonds against black velvet. The constellations seemed to look down on us, almost as if they cared for the small lives we lived beneath them.

For a moment, I felt like a child again, a child lost in a world far too vast to comprehend. And maybe, just maybe, that was another gift. The gift of ignorance. My hands shook, but I barely felt it. My fingers, clenched into fists, might as well have been someone else's. The whole time, I've been like this. Like I'm watching it all from a distance, numb to everything, to everyone.

But in that moment, as I looked at the stars, I realised something: I wasn't just numb. I've been lying to myself all this time, pretending I cared about the mission, the people, the cause. But deep down, I don't. The truth is, I crave the fight. The clash of steel, the sound of bones breaking beneath my hands. The destruction. I'm no better than the monster we're chasing.. The only thing that's real, the only thing that makes me feel anything, is the fight. The surge of adrenaline. The thrill when the sword bites flesh. Destruction. That's what pulls me back, time after time.

As I sat there, gazing into the fire, I couldn't help but wonder: could I ever find my way back? Or was this who I truly was?

The oracle had said my path was unstable, that I would face choices that could shape my destiny. Perhaps this was the first of those choices. I would need help. I wasn't strong enough to find the path on my own. I would swallow my pride, bow to those who thought themselves superior, use them as they used me. And maybe, just maybe, one day I would find my path. Maybe one day, I wouldn't feel like I was on the verge of breaking.

This wasn't hope. I wasn't that naïve. This was a goal. A target. Something I had to achieve.

As I lay my head down for one more night, I realised what I want. Yes, I found my new prey.

As I embraced this newfound outlook, something remarkable happened: all the worries, pain, and stress that had haunted me for as long as I could remember seemed to vanish. It was as if a heavy weight had been lifted from my shoulders. For the first time in what felt like an eternity, I was finally able to rest. That night, my mind was utterly still, no nightmares, no dreams, just pure, unbroken silence. And in that sleep, I found something I had been yearning for all my life: peace.

When I woke, however, I was greeted by three pairs of eyes staring at me, each one expressing a different level of curiosity. Perhaps they were surprised. It was the first time since we'd met that I had been the last one to wake. The peacefulness I had found in sleep was still with me, but it was unnerving. I wasn't used to it. It felt unfamiliar, but only for a fleeting moment. Before long, I felt a tugging at the corners of my lips. I was about to smile, but that tranquillity was shattered by a voice I enjoyed about as much as nails on a chalkboard.

"So, Sleeping Beauty finally awakens," mocked Rebecca. "We've been wasting time while waiting for you. Shawn over there won't let us do anything until our 'mythological expert' wakes up," she sneered, jerking her thumb in Shawn's direction. The annoyance in her tone was palpable as her eyes bore into me, daring me to respond.

"Well, I suppose I should thank you," I said, smirking slightly. "After all, I am the expert in all things mythological." I deliberately emphasised the word she had used to mock me, savouring the pettiness of the moment.

"Alright, you nerdy bastard," she began, but I interrupted her with a mischievous grin.

"Expert nerdy bastard," I corrected, enjoying the look of frustration that flashed across her face.

"Shut up and tell me what you think about finding this beast," she snapped, her irritation barely contained. Her arrogance grated on me. She acted as though she were in charge, though none of us had ever acknowledged her authority. Something inside me urged me to push back.

"Wait, do you want me to shut up, or do you want me to tell you?" I asked innocently, relishing the way her face slowly twisted into a mask of barely controlled hatred. Before she could retort, I cut her off again, my smile growing even wider. "The ophiotaurus is a sea creature, so it won't be far from bodies of water. Looking at the map, there are four large bodies of water in the area. I suggest we stick together and investigate them one by one."

For a brief moment, I held onto a flicker of hope that Rebecca would see reason. After all, what I was suggesting made perfect sense. But, as I had feared, my hopes were misplaced.

"This is exactly why I'm in charge," Rebecca chided. "I'll give you this: you know more about mythology than the rest of us. But sometimes, you're just so… unwise. It's showing, Hudson." She crossed her arms, glaring at me, clearly expecting some kind of response.

"Look, I get it. You are a true hunter. But trust me, following my lead is a win-win. Either we find the ophiotaurus, or you get to blame me if we don't. You're welcome." I explained with frustration.

Rebecca, unsatisfied, glanced at her sister for support. Anna, the quieter and more thoughtful of the two, hesitated for a moment before chiming in.

"I think what my sister is trying to say is that there are four of us and four rivers. We should split up and cover more ground," Anna said, her voice wavering ever so slightly. Was that hesitation I detected? Anna's hesitation spoke volumes. She was holding something back, that much was clear. It was a suggestion rife with danger, and I wasn't the only one who saw the flaw in her logic. Before I could say anything, Shawn spoke up, his voice tinged with anger.

"Do you want your sister to die, Rebecca?" he snapped, his fury barely concealed. "Do you honestly think there's nothing in this forest that could attack us? You want to send Anna, the healer, off on her own? Get off your high horse. Hudson usually has a reason for his madness."

I blinked, startled by Shawn's outburst. His rage surprised me,was he angry on my behalf, or had he simply had enough of Rebecca's bossy attitude? Either way, it seemed Shawn, usually the peacemaker, had finally lost his patience. His words hit Rebecca harder than I had expected. For a moment, her expression faltered, and I thought she might actually acknowledge her oversight. But the moment passed quickly, and before long, she and Shawn were locked in a heated argument, voices rising as they hurled insults at each other.

I wanted to pay attention to what they were saying, but my gaze was drawn to Anna.There was something about Anna's demeanour that didn't sit right. On the surface, she seemed detached, almost hollow. But her eyes, they glimmered with something else. Excitement? No, it wasn't that simple. Her gaze wasn't one of someone merely caught in the moment. It was as though she was taking in the chaos, savouring it. Why? What was she waiting for?

"Hudson, are you listening?" Shawn's voice snapped me back to reality.

"Uh, yeah," I mumbled, though I hadn't caught a word of what had been said. I had been too absorbed in my thoughts.

"We're splitting into two teams," Shawn explained, his annoyance apparent. "You're with me."

I shrugged nonchalantly. It didn't matter much to me whether we stayed together or split up. Either plan had its merits. But before I could move, Anna's voice broke the tension.

"Can I go with Hudson?" she asked quietly, surprising everyone. Her voice was small, almost timid, but there was a determination behind it. "I think everyone's a bit stressed, and maybe switching up the teams will help. Please, Bex."

Rebecca's mouth opened, but no words came out. She looked just as stunned as I felt. Anna volunteering to switch teams caught me off guard. It felt off. Like there was something else behind her eyes. But that's probably just my paranoia speaking. Ignore me.

After what felt like an eternity, Rebecca gave a slight nod of approval. Anna responded by quickly hugging her sister before hurrying over to me. As we began to move, I glanced back at Shawn and Rebecca. The fury in their eyes hadn't diminished. Their bloodlust was palpable, and I knew that this conflict was far from over.

As Anna and I walked away, I couldn't help but wonder what was going to happen next. The uneasy truce that held our group together felt like it was fraying at the seams. But for now, all I could do was focus on the task at hand, and try to understand the enigma walking beside me.

Chapter 17. "The least movement is of importance to all nature. The entire ocean is affected by a pebble.", Blaise Pascal

Shawn POV:

What just happened left me speechless. Truly, I can't even find the words to describe the mix of shock and frustration bubbling inside of me. The twins, who once seemed inseparable, as if their very souls were intertwined, have now split apart. And as if fate wanted to mock me, I ended up stuck with the worst one. I don't know how much more of her I can take.

Rebecca, the twin I'm stuck with, infuriates me beyond words. At first, I tried to be gentle. I tried to be patient, even understanding. I thought perhaps there were things in her past, traumas I couldn't grasp, that justified her behaviour. But no. Nothing excuses the way she acts. She's beyond reason, beyond empathy. I can't even begin to understand how the trials of this tutorial, as gruelling as they have been, twisted her into the person standing next to me now.

In the beginning, she was wary of all of us, suspicious of our every move. Honestly, I didn't blame her at the time. I was probably even worse. It took me a long time to trust Hudson, and even now, I can't say I fully do. But there's a difference. Despite all my doubts, I've grown to respect Hudson in some strange way. He's reliable, even if he's not the easiest person to deal with. But Rebecca? You couldn't pay me enough to respect her anymore.

She's grown more spiteful as the tutorial progressed, and I just don't understand it.

We saved her. We pulled her out of a nightmare, and yet she doesn't even have the basic human decency to say thank you. Instead, she acts as if we're just as bad as those who would harm her. And don't even get me started on how she treats Hudson. He may not be perfect, but the way she provokes him is uncalled for. Of course, Hudson doesn't help the situation, he eggs her on, almost as if he's looking for a fight. I wish he could just be the bigger person, but that's not who he is, and I guess that's rubbed off on me now, too.

We've been wandering through this forsaken margrave for nearly two hours. The once-beautiful landscape now feels oppressive, the vibrant greens and shimmering waters somehow more suffocating than serene. My shoes are soaked through with the filth of the ground, each step more agonising than the last. My legs ache, my feet drag, and yet the worst part isn't the discomfort, it's the silence. It's the unspoken tension between us, so thick it's practically tangible.

I've spent the entire time walking on eggshells, doing everything in my power to keep the peace. Rebecca wanted to lead, so I let her. She wanted me to shut up, so I did. Not because I wanted to keep her happy, but because I didn't want to stir up any more trouble. But now, I've had enough. Enough of the silence. Enough of pretending. Enough of her.

I finally broke the silence, not because I cared what she thought, but because I needed to hear something, anything that wasn't the sound of our feet squelching through the mud. "If we find the beast, what do you want to do?" I asked, knowing full well I wouldn't like the answer.

Rebecca, in true form, responded with the arrogance I've come to expect from her. "Obviously, I'm going to kill it," she said, her voice dripping with pride. "Just imagine having the power to end the gods themselves. I'll rule better than any of them ever could. Of course, I'll spare my patron out of respect, but I'll show them what it means to be a true queen."

Her words hit me like a blow to the chest, my mind reeling from the gravity of her madness. "You're mad," I said, hoping,foolishly,that my words would get through to her. "You're absolutely mad."

She turned her bow on me, her eyes blazing with fury. "You wouldn't understand," she hissed. "I don't want to just survive. I want to thrive. I want to be better than any man could ever be. And for now, you're useful. Don't push your luck."

Her words stunned me. I had known for a while that Rebecca was ambitious, but this? This was something else entirely. Her desire to rise above the gods wasn't just reckless, it was dangerous. The creature we sought wasn't just another beast to be slain. If we found it, if she gained the power she sought, the consequences would be catastrophic.

I couldn't stay silent any longer. "Rebecca, I've had enough of your delusions. What makes you think you'll be any better than the gods who have ruled for aeons? They are gods for a reason! What makes you think you'll be a better ruler than them?"

She didn't hesitate. "Because I know," she snarled. "They've always been immortal. They were born with that power. They can't possibly understand what it means to be mortal, to suffer, to strive for something greater. They sit in their thrones, blind to the world's misery. I can be better than them because I've lived through the suffering they ignore."

Her naivety was staggering. "Do you really think you'll be any different once you have that power?" I shot back. "Look at Heracles. He attained godhood, but his most famous deeds were from when he was still a demigod. Once he became a god, he did nothing of significance. There are minor gods like Morpheus, Iris and Aeolus who are more important in the realm of the gods than Heracles ever was, despite being weaker. You'll be no different."

Her response was swift and violent. An arrow whizzed past my head, grazing my ear. I froze, staring at her in disbelief.

"Shawn," she said coldly, "don't you dare compare me to a man of such little calibre. If you dare to, the next arrow won't miss."

I stood there, stunned into silence, as she glared at me, her blue eyes ablaze with fury. We continued walking, the silence between us even more unbearable than before. My mind raced, trying to process what had just happened. I had known Rebecca was dangerous, but this was something else. She was on a path I couldn't follow, a path that could lead to the destruction of everything we had worked for.

We trudged through the swamp for another hour, the oppressive silence weighing down on us like a physical force. My feet felt like lead, each step harder than the last. Just when I thought I couldn't take it anymore, I saw it, the creature we had been searching for.

It was more beautiful than I could have imagined. It waded through the water with a grace that seemed otherworldly, its scales catching the light and refracting it in a stunning array of colours. It moved with a quiet elegance, as if it belonged to the very sea itself. I could feel the love it had for the ocean, and I could sense that the ocean loved it in return.

But before I could fully take in the sight, Rebecca charged at it, her bow drawn and an arrow ready. The beast, sensing the danger, let out a mournful sound, a low, pleading moo that tugged at something deep inside me.

For the first time since we started this journey, I felt genuine sorrow for something that wasn't human.

The beast knew its fate. Hudson had told me that the Ophiotaurus only had value in death, and it seemed the creature was all too aware of that fact. It didn't fight back. It ran. And in that moment, I tried to stop Rebecca. I yelled at her to wait, to think. But it was too late. She fired her arrow, and in the blink of an eye, the Ophiotaurus was gone, vanishing into the depths once again.

As I stood there, staring at the empty water where the beast had been, a sinking feeling settled in my chest. I knew then that this was just the beginning. Rebecca's thirst for power wouldn't end with the Ophiotaurus. And if we didn't stop her, there would be no end to the destruction she would leave in her wake.

Hudson's POV:

Perplexed. That was the word that kept surfacing. I didn't understand why Anna was here. Alone. With me. Her sister is always at her side, until now.

She hadn't stumbled into this. She'd chosen it.

We walked without speaking for a while, the rhythm of our footsteps quietly in sync. I kept glancing at her, but she never seemed to notice.

Then, lightly:

"So, Hudson," she said, as though she'd only just thought of it, "do you dislike me?"

It wasn't said with an edge. If anything, it sounded curious, as though she were asking whether the tea had too much sugar.

I blinked. "No," I said. Then, after a beat: "Why?"

She shrugged. "Just a feeling. You tend to go quiet around me." A faint smile. "I figured I'd ask before I invented a whole narrative."

I gave a vague nod, noncommittal. "You don't strike me as someone who needs to invent much."

"Oh, I do," she said cheerfully. "Otherwise life's too boring."

That got a small exhale of breath from me, half amusement, half wariness. "And your sister? Does she know that?"

Anna's expression didn't shift. "She knows me better than anyone." She tilted her head slightly. "But I suppose that's not what you were asking."

I didn't answer.

She let the silence hang. Then, gently: "If you're worried about her and Shawn, you don't have to be. She listens to me."

I made a small sound. Noncommittal again. "And do you not think this will end badly?"

She considered it. "He's harmless relax"

The phrasing caught me off guard. Not yes, not no. Not even vague approval. Just... a sidestep, wrapped in something that sounded like wisdom.

She kept walking, hands folded behind her back, as though we were on a garden stroll and not tracking a creature that could tear us apart.

"I wanted to talk to you," she added, as if remembering. "You're not easy to get a read on."

"That a problem?" I asked.

"No." She looked over, faint amusement in her eyes. "Just makes things more interesting."

I didn't know what that meant. Still don't.

A breeze passed. Anna glanced up, scanning the treeline, then back at me.

"Do you know what you want to do?" she asked. "After all this?"

I frowned. "All this?"

She gestured vaguely. "The tutorial. The gods. The rest of it."

I hesitated. "Why are you asking?"

Her voice stayed light. "Because it's easier to work with someone if you know what they're aiming for."

I watched her carefully. Her tone was even, her expression open. It could've been sincerity. It could've been anything.

"I'm figuring it out," I said finally.

She smiled, small and warm. "Same."

The conversation drifted from there, back to the Ophiotaurus, to logistics, to guesses and strategies and trivial things. She didn't press further, and I didn't offer.

Still, a part of me stayed alert, the way you might in a room that feels just a little too quiet.

As if in answer to my unspoken plea, a ripple broke the surface of a nearby pond. There, standing in the shallow water, was the Ophiotaurus, a magnificent creature, every bit as majestic as the myths had described. I approached cautiously, knowing that any sudden movements would only serve to agitate it.

I knew the myths. The Ophiotaurus was said to possess incredible power, but myths are only half-truths. They're based in fact but are far from concrete reality. With my sword drawn and Anna close behind me, I stepped toward the beast. But then, something in its eyes caught my attention, fear.

I realised my mistake immediately and sheathed my blade, holding my hands open to show I meant no harm. But the fear didn't leave its eyes. It wasn't just reacting to the sword. Perhaps it recognized something in me, something darker, something I had only recently begun to understand about myself.

Approaching the Ophiotaurus was a gamble, one wrong move and we could be caught in an endless spiral of conflict. But it wasn't just the creature that concerned me; it was Anna. While I calculated a way forward, her hand lightly touched my shoulder, halting me. In that moment, it wasn't just about calming the beast. She wanted to show me she was in control, not just of the situation, but of me. I let her think she had that power, but my thoughts were already turning, looking for the cracks in her armour. She moved gracefully, like this was the most natural thing in the world. Within seconds, the beast had calmed, resting its great head against her palm.

I had to give her credit,she was full of surprises.

Beep!
The Ophiotaurus has been found!

Contribution:
1. ***Anna Harris (50%)***
2. ***Hudson Mitchell (30%)***
3. ***Shawn Addams (20%)***
4. ***Rebecca Harris (10%)***

Rewards have been allocated.

Two losses in the span of 6 hours, how fun. Before I could check my status we were teleported immediately to the waiting area.

Chapter 18. "A house divided against itself cannot stand." – Abraham Lincoln

We were met by the king, his malevolent grin sending a chill down my spine. His eyes curved upward, brimming with expectation, as his gaze pierced deep into our souls, saturating the air with an atmosphere of malice. I faced him, resolute and breathless, waiting for his command to speak, longing for the moment when we could finally breathe freely. Yet, it seemed one of our party, ever too self-important, spoke out of turn.

"Oi, Your Majesty," Rebecca blurted, her tone dripping with sarcasm. Can you explain how I had the least contribution in this quest?" she challenged, her voice dripping with the kind of arrogance that dared him to disagree. The king's gaze turned icy, a muscle twitching in his jaw as if he were envisioning her head mounted on a stake, a testament to her foolishness. The silent fury that enveloped us was palpable, a bloodlust tightening around our throats. Still, Rebecca stood her ground, a defiant glare in her eyes as if daring the king to challenge her misplaced confidence. Seething with rage yet bound by the rules of this realm, he finally began to speak.

"Rebecca Harris," he said, his voice steady, "I know not what the fates have decreed. I know not what you believe you have accomplished. Any answer I give will merely reflect my professional and personal reasoning. Is that satisfactory to you?" His unexpected politeness was disconcerting; it felt as if he was placing Rebecca on a precarious pedestal, a foundation destined to crumble. He relished this moment, deriving pleasure from her impending downfall. This was the king revealing his true nature.

After a deliberate pause, he continued, "It's actually somewhat humorous, your hubris. You claim you do not deserve this lowly position, yet all your actions point to it. From the beginning, you believed this quest was designed for you, yet you never questioned whether that was truly the case. Your arrogance will be your undoing. It prevented you from accepting guidance from others and listening to allies when victory was within your grasp. Your failure to acknowledge your comrades' concerns, which led them to the right conclusion, speaks volumes. So, tell me honestly: do you truly believe you deserve the top position? Perhaps the loss of stats will teach you a valuable lesson. You will be the only one left unrewarded. I hope you learn today."

The king's gaze turned towards Rebecca, as if she were nothing more than a bothersome fly. Rage flickered across her face as she scanned the room, her envy and anger palpable, even directed at her own sister. Yet, the worst part was the clear dismissal of his words.

The deities are interested in this conversation.

"Rebecca Harris," he continued, his tone shifting to a more personal note, "that was my professional opinion. Now I shall share my personal thoughts, so heed my words. You are vermin, the lowest of the low. Your mere presence irritates me. The fact that you are even in this temple is a stain on my Lady's image. How dare you stand here, in Her holy grounds? I wish nothing but the worst upon you. You are fortunate that the system permits me to allocate punishments only for the first two floors; you will still be rewarded on the others. But heed this: the system is far cruller than I. You will answer to me before you assess what has befallen you. Do you understand?"

As he finished his tirade, disgust painted his face, the silence around us thickening until it was shattered by the cawing of a crow. "This is absolute bullshit, and you know it!" I recognized the look on Rebecca's face, embarrassment turned to aggression. "You? Punish me? How dare you! Need I remind you that you're here due to your Lady? I will not have this disgrace attached to my name. Perhaps it's your Lady who made the mistake." In that moment, she sealed her fate.

A certain deity relinquishes potential patronage

"You dare?… YOU DARE BESMIRCH LADY ATHENA'S NAME!" he spat, his voice a low growl, each word dripping with venom that pierced the silence like a blade. "Her grace is beyond description, her presence unmatched. Yet you have the audacity to question her very dominion? Do you wish to share the fate of those who've crossed me before? Enough. Olympus, since I cannot punish her, I implore your assistance. Use your almighty power to punish her!"

The Greek pantheon has heard the plea.
Olympus is voting.
...
Voting has concluded.
10 for.
1 against
1 abstained.
The system has decided the punishment.
Enacting now.

Without warning, a horrendous screech erupted from my left. Rebecca writhed in agony, her pain visceral and horrifying. I watched as her arm contorted, her shirt ripping apart, revealing the gruesome reality beneath. Muscles twisted, tearing from tendons with a sickening sound, a crack that sent shockwaves through her body, robbing her of her ability to scream. She collapsed, bones protruding grotesquely from her flesh. But the worst part, the utter lack of blood, was inhumane, surreal, and unfathomable. I blinked, momentarily dazed, and when I opened my eyes, it was gone. The arm had vanished, as if it had never existed, and a message appeared to notify us of the dire situation.

Rebecca Harris has offended those who are dearly loved by the system. She has offended the great council of one of the most powerful pantheons. As per their request, we decided to remove her right arm painfully, as a right handed archer she will now be unable to shoot unless she ascends to mortal aspirant. In order to maintain balance we will give F ranked

throwing knives so she is still able to embody the spirit of an archer.

An Olympian Goddess wishes to relay a message.
Permission granted.
Displaying now:
"A maiden who does not know how to accept her shortcomings is not worthy of becoming one of my huntresses, a shame, I had high hopes for this one. I enjoyed this particular punishment, despite losing a new archer. My brother also is jumping with joy from this."
Lady Artemis, Goddess of the Hunt, Wild Animals, The Moon, Nature, Chastity, Childbirth, Fertility, Health, Archery, Virginity, Sacred Groves and Springs, Protector of the Innocent, and Agriculture.

This news was shocking to us all, mostly Rebecca of course, but I couldn't help but grin as I saw her overconfident facade crumble away. The king left and simply told us he couldn't bear to be in the same room as Rebecca. The most surprising of all was Anna. She consoled her sister, but her eyes were void of any empathy. I wonder how long she has been playing this game.

Thankfully the silence lasted long enough for me to check my status.

Name: Hudson Mitchell
Rank: Mortal (F)
Class: Light Warrior
Patron #1: N/A
Patron #2: N/A
Patron #3: N/A

Skills:

- **Identify Level 1 [A]**
- **Low Pain Resistance Level 8 [P]**
- **Predatorial Vision Level 9 [A]**
- **Chaotic Battle Instinct Level 5 [A]**

Before I could revel in my newfound abilities I noticed there was one notification I have yet to read.

New Item.

Grippy Vambraces (F)

Crafted by Creidhne, the Celtic god of metalwork, when he was a kid and kept dropping things in his forge. These vambraces were made for those with *beastly instincts*,or at least, that's what the myths say. In reality, they were just meant to help him hold onto his tools without burning himself. They give a small boost to grip and strength, like enough to lift a heavy barrel or wrestle a sheep,but don't expect to tear through steel. They've got that weird, sticky feel, probably from all the random animal hides and old forge dust used to make them. Also, they smell faintly of wet fur. Super practical.

"Thank the heavens for this," I muttered, relief washing over me as I wore them. Now, I possess three items to my name. But I needed a sword, a weapon I desperately craved, yet the system persistently denied me. Each prayer for a blade went unanswered, and the sting of that rejection gnawed at my pride. I had come to terms with my identity and glimpsed the path before me, but one truth remained unwavering: I needed a sword.

As I pondered my plight, my colleagues began to read their status updates. Anna, with her characteristic cheer, offered a suggestion to lighten the mood. "Hey Bex, why don't we announce our items? So you don't feel bad." I was taken aback by her tone; it was genuine, but surely she couldn't be that naïve. Did she truly lack the empathy to recognize her sister's potential distress?

Shawn, ever perceptive, spoke up first. "Um, Anna? I hate to say this, but don't you think announcing items might actually upset your sister, especially if she's the lowest among us?" He watched as a smile crept onto Anna's face, oblivious to the tension she was creating.

"I appreciate your concern, Shawn," she replied, resting a hand reassuringly on his arm, "but my intention is to show Bex that catching up isn't as hard as it seems." Her delicate smile lit her fair features, and she gestured toward Rebecca, whose mood was evidently fragile. "Go ahead, Bex. Share your items."

"Arrows and knives " Rebecca murmured, her voice barely above a whisper.

"A cloak, and gloves" Anna declared confidently.

"I got a chestguard and boots," Shawn added, puffing out his chest with pride.

Their gazes turned to me, expectant and probing. I felt the weight of their scrutiny, a palpable tension in the air as if they were waiting for a cue to a game I didn't want to play. Anna's deceit hung heavy between us; I could see the false bravado in her eyes. Would lying about my own level provide me with temporary safety, or would it merely deepen the rift between us?

For a fleeting moment, doubt crept in. Would it be so terrible to bend the truth, to shield myself from their judgement? But no. I wouldn't compromise my integrity for their comfort. The thought of fabricating a lie twisted in my gut. I'd rather stand alone, swordless and exposed, than kneel before their expectations.

If my honesty painted me as the enemy, then so be it. I would bear that label with pride, for I was no weakling to hide behind deception. The truth was my armour, even if it left me vulnerable. I would forge my own path, one built on the strength of authenticity, no matter how daunting the journey ahead.

Your Potential Patron is proud of your vigilance and pride.

"Pauldrons, boots, and vambraces," I stated, watching as their reactions unfolded. Anna feigned indifference, likely relieved to find herself close to my level. Shawn beamed at me, a glint of excitement in his eyes as if eager for the rivalry I had unwittingly created. Then there was Rebecca, whose contempt was palpable. My victory hurt her pride, and I felt a mischievous urge to stoke that fire, relishing the chaos of the moment.

Your potential patron is proud of both your vigilance and pride.

"See, Rebecca? You have 2 items, I have 3," I said, forcing a playful frown. "Unfortunately, that's what happens when you go against your superiors." My words dripped with intentional malice, but I also wanted to gauge Anna's reaction. If she truly wished to play the role of the caring sister, she would chastise me.

"Hudson, you need to rein it in. Don't tease my sister," Anna responded, her voice firm but then faltering as she continued, "but you do have a point, Bex. It's not wise to challenge a demigod of a king." There it was; she had walked straight into my trap.

Shawn, troubled by my taunt, chimed in, "Hey man, that was a bit rude, not gonna lie."

I seized the opportunity to amplify the tension. "Nah, it's just funny." I let out a laugh, delighting in her misfortune.

Just as Shawn was about to retort, the king reentered the room, his presence a force that dwarfed us all. He looked down upon us as if we were mere vermin, perhaps sharing my sentiment: vermin belong among vermin. He

144

paused over me for a moment, his gaze weighing heavily before he spoke.

"I hope you all grasp the gravity of our situation," he boomed, his voice echoing throughout the chamber. "To think you will need to escape my merciless palace alongside someone who can barely keep their balance... Well, consider yourselves fortunate. No weapons will be allowed on this floor." With a resonant laugh and a single snap of his fingers, we were whisked away once again.

Chapter 19. "A ship is safe in harbour, but that's not what ships are for." , John A. Shedd.

The first thing we noticed was the smell, a murky, rotten stench that clung to the air like a suffocating shroud. It surrounded us, relentless and inescapable, a stark contrast to the pristine environment of the previous floor. The king was toying with us, testing our resolve. The walls were riddled with corpses, some fresh, others decayed beyond recognition. It was a grim reminder of what awaited us if we faltered.

This was the floor of traps, a labyrinth of deception steeped in cruelty. I knew I had to warn the others. Without vigilance, we'd meet our end before even realizing what had gone wrong.

"We need to be careful," I began, my voice steady despite the unease gnawing at me. "Carelessness will lead us to ruin. This is the trap floor, and we have no idea what's waiting for us."

The others nodded solemnly, and we began our search. The maze was alive, the cracks in the walls seemed to watch us, mocking our every cautious step. Seconds blurred into minutes, minutes stretched into hours, and after what felt like a day, it became evident that we'd made no real progress.

"This is ridiculous," Shawn finally snapped, frustration bleeding into his voice. "We've been treading as carefully as possible, and we've barely scratched the surface of this damn maze."

Anna, ever the agitator, chimed in without hesitation. "Shawn's right, Hudson. This little game of yours has gone on long enough. We need to pick up the pace or starve to death in this hellhole. Quit overthinking and trust your instincts."

Anna's bluntness was as grating as her logic was sound. Her peculiar reasoning often pushed me to my limits, not because she was wrong but because she had a knack for being infuriatingly correct. And now, she has backed me into a corner. Pride urged me to resist, but even my stubbornness couldn't ignore the cold reality spelled out by the system's latest update:

Time Limit Introduced.
Time Used: 8 hours
Time Remaining: 12 hours
Distance Traveled: 11 km
Distance Remaining: 89 km

I had no choice but to relent. Even the system was mocking my slow and steady approach. Resigned, I stepped back, watching as Shawn took the lead. Anna's smug expression only deepened my irritation. To my chagrin, their approach worked. In just three hours, we'd covered six kilometers, bypassing traps with an almost insulting ease. My cautious method had failed, and their impulsive strategy had proven me wrong.

I silently wished for more dangerous traps,not out of malice, but to validate my earlier stance. Or so I told myself. But as the thought lingered, a chilling realization crept in: Was I truly wishing harm upon my allies for the sake of pride? The idea disgusted me, yet I couldn't shake it.

As if answering my unspoken prayers, a deafening metallic roar shattered the uneasy silence. Serrated blades erupted from the walls, spinning at incomprehensible speeds, pausing briefly as if savoring our fear. Then, without warning, they lunged.

This wasn't a trap we could outsmart or sidestep. It was a predator, designed to kill. The blades seemed alive, their teeth chattering with glee, feeding off our terror. We ran, our breaths ragged, our footsteps heavy, and yet we couldn't shake the feeling of being hunted. This was the first time in my life I truly felt like prey.

"What the fuck triggered this?!" I screamed, desperation clawing at my voice.

"I hit a button!" Shawn admitted, his voice trembling. "I thought charging ahead was better than creeping along. I'm sorry!"

If I hadn't been consumed by fear, I might have pitied him. But in that moment, all I could think was, *pathetic.*

Minutes stretched like hours as we fled, and when the cacophony of the blades finally ceased, we collapsed in exhaustion. Fury burned within me.

"Why the hell did you do that, Shawn?" I demanded.

"What do you mean?" he shot back. "All the traps so far have been easy! How was I supposed to know they'd get worse?"

Before I could respond, the fallen archer cut in, her voice icy and laced with venom. "How were you supposed to know? Are you serious? I've lost an arm, for fuck's sake! Do you honestly think barreling through traps without a plan is a good idea? Enough. We can't trust your instincts anymore."

This revision sharpens the narrative, heightens tension, and deepens character development while maintaining the original tone. Let me know if you'd like further adjustments!

Her words hit me harder than I cared to admit. She was right. Shawn's recklessness wasn't the sole issue here, it was my failure. I'd been so determined to dictate our pace, so insistent on caution, that I'd ignored the reality of our situation. My supposed strategy wasn't just slowing us down; it was killing our morale. And worse, it had revealed something dark within me.

Why had I silently prayed for more dangerous traps? Why had I wanted my colleagues to falter so I could be vindicated? The thought churned in my stomach like poison. Pride. That insidious beast had wormed its way into my mind, clouding my judgment. I had preached vigilance to my team, not to keep us safe, but to prove myself right. And now, we were paying the price for my hubris.

But her voice wasn't just a reprimand; it was a wake-up call. As I sat there, staring at the flickering torches that lined the walls, a realization dawned on me. I had been relying too much on logic, analyzing each step, weighing every decision as if I could outthink this labyrinth. But this maze wasn't built to be solved by intellect alone. It demanded something primal,something instinctual.

I thought back to the traps we had encountered so far. They weren't just puzzles; they were predators. The way the saw blades had paused before lunging, the way the walls seemed to watch us,they weren't random designs. They were crafted to elicit fear, to exploit hesitation. And in that moment, I understood: this wasn't a game of intellect. This was a hunt.

If we were to survive, I couldn't simply be cautious or methodical. I had to become a predator myself, someone who could read danger and react instinctively. My heart pounded as the pieces began to fall into place. This was why I had struggled to keep pace with the others. I had ignored the very skill that set me apart: my ability to sense and adapt to threats without overthinking. It wasn't just about moving faster; it was about embracing the instincts I had suppressed for so long.

But embracing them wouldn't be easy. Instinct wasn't a switch I could flip,it was something I had to surrender to. My mind raced, balancing the risk and reward of what I was about to do. If I let myself fall into that primal state for too long, I risked losing control, blurring the line between calculation and chaos. Yet, if I didn't, we wouldn't make it through this floor alive.

I raised my hands slowly, demanding the attention of the group. The argument between Shawn and the archer died down as their eyes locked onto mine. The tension was palpable, every second stretched thin by the weight of expectation. I closed my eyes and exhaled, allowing the noise of the world to fade. This wasn't about them anymore; it was about me, and whether I could accept what needed to be done.

Then, in the silence, I let go. My vision darkened, my senses sharpened, and I steeled myself to activate my *Predatorial Vision* for the longest stretch yet. This wasn't just a skill,it was my lifeline, the only way forward. Whatever this maze threw at us next, I would be ready.

The first thought that came to my mind was *weird.* I don't really know how to explain it. Up until this point I only used *Predatorial Vision* as a form of attack. A way to strike at opponents. A way to find weaknesses that they did not even know that they had. The weakness lesser beings had, the weakness of prey. But then again what does that make me? When I took caution for every step, where I was worried about falling victim to the traps, where I was worried about the saw blades reaching their target and chewing me alive. No that's not true. That's a lie to myself. I was not worried. Not in the slightest. I was... scared. I was scared that I would become what I once was at 12 years old. Something that I swore to throw aside. Something that I vowed to burn. A memory that I myself had forgotten. But it seems my body didn't. That damn room. That fucking shitty prison cell. Designed to break adults with its simple yet effective structure. THAT CELL. That cell. Yeah it was in that cell that I realised how harrowing, how terrifying the world truly is. That cell was where I lost any hopefulness of a happy childhood.

The fact is, this entire labyrinth, from the moment I stepped into it, was mocking me. Athena, the goddess of wisdom. She was looking down on us instinctual types, much like her relationship with the true god of war. It was as if she had an inbuilt hatred of those who trusted their guts more than their intelligence, and unfortunately for me, this labyrinth was reminding me of that at every twist and turn.

This fucking level kept poking at the insecurity I thought I had long since conquered, yet it remained. Scarred so deep into the flesh of my soul that the very foundation was shaking. I hated this feeling. Why did I still feel like prey when I escaped that hell? I was angry, livid even. I get that she was an Olympian, the favored princess of Olympus, but that's it. A deity who picked favorites far too easily. Someone who did not even consider the benefits some mere mortal might have. But I had to steel myself. I opened my mouth and decided to open a topic that had been hidden for far too long.

"Guys, we need to talk," I started, my voice steady but sharp. The stereotypical opening to every uncomfortable conversation.

"What's going on, man?" Shawn asked, his brows furrowing slightly, his tone cautious.

His broad shoulders slumped ever so slightly, betraying the weight he carried. Rebecca stood slightly behind him, her bow slung across her back, her empty left sleeve pinned neatly at the shoulder. Her sharp blue eyes scanned me as if trying to dissect my intentions. Anna, the healer, stood quietly to the side, her soft smile carefully hiding something sharper underneath.

I took a step forward, letting my onyx eyes sweep across them. They reflected not their strengths, but their weaknesses,cracks in their armor, insecurities hidden beneath brave facades.

"I don't believe any of you are capable of leading anymore." My voice was cold, resolute. "I want to give another attempt and lead us to the end of this shitty floor."

The words hung in the air, heavy as stone. I let my eyes linger on Anna, the so-called healer of the group. She wore a smile,not warm, not comforting, but sharp and knowing. And then, just for a fraction of a second, something changed in her gaze. A flicker of intensity, an almost predatory sharpness. It was like staring into a mirror,a predator sizing up another.

153

But it was gone in an instant, leaving behind the carefully constructed image of the kind-hearted healer. I couldn't help but smirk at the facade.

"I promise," I continued, my tone softening, "if within two hours we don't cover at least three kilometers, you can all strip me of this role. But even if you don't trust me, I will still hold myself responsible. So if you don't trust me or my leadership, trust my promise."

Silence followed. Not the calm kind,this was heavy, oppressive. I could see the gears turning in their heads, the silent weighing of risks and rewards.

Shawn scratched at his beard, a nervous tick he always fell back on when pressured. Rebecca's piercing gaze stayed locked on me, her lips pressed into a thin line. Anna's smile had vanished, replaced by an unreadable expression.

I wanted them to believe me, not because I needed validation, but because I needed them to *move*. Forward. Together. I wasn't asking for blind trust, just a chance.

Then, like the crack of thunder in a still sky, Shawn spoke.

"Guys, I fucked up."

Rebecca snorted, rolling her eyes. "Of course you did, you melon."

"Point is," Shawn pushed on, his voice louder now, "I no longer want to be the one to lead us through this. I'm scared, alright? And hey, he promised, didn't he? He hasn't broken a promise yet."

I blinked. When did I make promises before this? Apparently, I had. Shawn seemed so certain of it, and Rebecca and Anna were nodding along as if my word was gospel. It was almost funny. My word? Trustworthy? If my old 'friends' could see me now, they'd die laughing.

But Shawn's declaration had cracked something in the group dynamic. The tension eased, if only slightly, and a reluctant consensus began to form.

"Fine," Rebecca said at last, her voice tight with irritation. "But if you screw this up, I'm feeding you to whatever horror Athena's got waiting for us in this hellhole."

"Duly noted," I said dryly.

Anna finally spoke, her voice soft but firm. "We'll follow. But don't think for a second we'll hold back if you lead us into a death trap."

"Fair enough," I replied.

The labyrinth stretched before us, an endless corridor of shadows and faint torchlight. The oppressive air pressed down on my chest, but I took the first step. And then another. My comrades followed, the sound of their footsteps blending with the faint hum of something ancient lurking in the dark.

I kept my eyes peeled, my senses heightened to the point of paranoia. The labyrinth wasn't just a physical obstacle,it was psychological warfare. Every corner felt like a trap, every shadow a dagger aimed at our backs.

"Do you think she's watching us?" Shawn asked softly, his voice trembling.

"Athena? Of course she is," Rebecca replied. "Gods don't build mazes like this just to ignore the people stupid enough to walk into them."

"Stupid enough, huh?" I muttered.

Rebecca smirked faintly, but it didn't reach her eyes. We walked in silence for a while longer until we reached a junction. Three paths split before us, each more foreboding than the last.

"Which way?" Shawn asked.

I closed my eyes, letting my instincts take over. I wasn't Athena. I wasn't wise, logical, or strategic. But I trusted my gut. It has gotten me this far.

"Left," I said firmly.

"Left it is," Rebecca muttered.

We turned as one, stepping into yet another dark corridor. My heartbeat echoed in my ears, but I kept walking.

Somewhere, deep in the unseen corners of this labyrinth, I could almost hear laughter,sharp, feminine, and condescending.

Athena was watching, alright. And she was waiting for me to fail.

But she would have to wait a little longer. Because I wasn't stopping now.

Chapter 20."In a world of imperfect choices, wisdom lies in selecting the option that leads to the least suffering." , Epictetus.

The moment we stepped through the left path, a putrid smell slithered its way into our nostrils, as if a titanoboa was slowly constricting me, squeezing the air from my lungs and robbing me of one of my most valued senses. The oppressive smell danced at our unease, shifting in its intensity but only growing fouler with each passing second. It felt alive, like a cruel entity savoring our discomfort. In a moment of desperation, I made the fatal mistake of opening my mouth to breathe.

The taste that followed was beyond horrific. Words barely scratched the surface of its vileness. But if I were to try, imagine being a child again, forced to eat something you abhorred. You sit there at the dinner table, staring at the plate as if it holds radioactive waste. Your mother watches you with a smile that tries to be comforting, but your mind warps it into something oppressive,not out of her anger, but from your own growing fear.

Eventually, you cave. Trembling hands lift the spoon to your mouth, and the dreaded food slides across your tongue. Its slimy texture fights your throat every step of the way, but you swallow, desperate to end the experience. You don't taste it; you endure it. But the aftertaste remains, stubborn and vile, taunting you long after the bite is gone. And when your stomach finally rebels, when you find yourself bent over the toilet, retching up the meal and replacing the aftertaste of the food with the acrid sting of bile... somehow, inexplicably, the vomit tastes better.

Do you remember that feeling? Multiply it tenfold, then toss it into the abyss of Tartarus. That's what it felt like to breathe in this cursed corridor. And yet, we had no choice but to keep moving forward, forced to endure each wretched breath. I silently prayed that, if I ever got stronger, breathing would become optional.

"Hudson, you fucking asshole!" Rebecca's voice cut through the darkness behind me, sharp and angry. I could hear her footsteps approaching, heavy with frustration. But something was odd. I could feel her presence behind me, not just hear her, but *feel* her. How? **Predatorial Vision** was supposed to enhance my sight, not my sense of touch or presence.

A faint, high-pitched bell rang in my ears. I shook my head, trying to dispel the noise, and focused back on our path.

The corridor stretched out before us, a serpentine maze shrouded in oppressive darkness. It was thick, tangible, like a living shadow pressing down on us, herding us backward with invisible hands. My skill, my so-called advantage, felt useless here. I had activated Predatorial Vision with smug confidence, thinking myself clever, but now I could almost hear Athena laughing at me from some celestial throne. How foolish of me to think I could outwit a goddess.

And then, amidst the choking blackness, I saw it,a glimmer of gold, faint but unmistakable. My eyes locked onto it. It felt surreal, like a mirage in a desert. I took a step forward, drawn toward it, but an invisible force slammed against me, halting my movement entirely.

"What the hell?" I whispered, gritting my teeth as another bell rang softly in my ears.

"Guys, can you see that? The gold light?" I called out behind me.

A chorus of agreement followed.

"Wait, Hudson," Rebecca spoke again, her voice softer now, cautious. "Is this... is this a guide? Like some kind of sign?"

"I don't know. Rebecca, can you try moving toward it?"

She stepped past me without hesitation, her confidence almost infuriating. But then, as she moved forward, I felt it again,the force pulling at me, and the ringing in my ears growing sharper.

Instinctively, I reached out and grabbed her wrist.

"Hey! What the hell?" she snapped, wrenching her arm free. "I'm not into guys, Hudson, back off!"

I held up my hands in surrender. "Calm down. Just... was there a force stopping you? Did you feel anything?"

She hesitated, then shook her head. "No. Nothing."

"Let me try," Rebecca's healer twin chimed in, stepping forward. As she passed me, I grabbed her arm, and the bell rang again.

"Hey, Hudson, man," Shawn spoke up, his voice low and wary. "Don't you think this might be a guide? Like a checkpoint or something?"

But the ringing, the pulling sensation, it was screaming at me now. It wasn't a guide. It wasn't salvation.

"No," I said firmly. "It's not a guide. It's a trap. A false grace. Everyone, grab hands. Now."

Groans of reluctance filled the air, but eventually, everyone complied. One by one, we linked hands, forming an unsteady chain in the oppressive dark. I could feel the weight of their trust resting heavily on my shoulders, and I pushed forward.

The golden glimmers taunted us, whispering promises of safety, of rest, of warmth. The shadows seemed to breathe around us, pressing closer, their murmurings like a lullaby. My eyelids feel heavy. My legs are weak. A deep, bone-weary exhaustion seeped into my muscles.

Rest, the shadows whispered. *You deserve it. Just close your eyes. Stop walking. Stop...*

No.

I grit my teeth and squeezed my eyes shut. The darkness was clever, weaponizing our exhaustion, our weaknesses. I forced one foot in front of the other, dragging the chain of teammates behind me.

"Keep walking!" I barked, my voice cracking with effort. "Don't stop! Don't listen to it!"

And then, a break. A faint light, this time clear and warm, broke through the shadows.

"There!" I choked out. "We're almost there! Keep moving!"

The air shifted. The oppressive force pushing against us began to wane, and suddenly, we stumbled into an open space. A dim, flickering light illuminated the room, a lantern set atop a cracked stone pedestal.

We had made it.

The group spread out, catching their breath. Rebecca leaned against a nearby wall, her arms crossed, her expression tight but relieved.

"Okay," I said, exhaling slowly. "Five minutes. Just... five minutes to get our bearings."

No one argued. No one complained. For five minutes, we stood in silence, gathering our strength, staring into the flickering lantern light. And for now, that was enough.

Before we could even properly catch our breath, a notification rang through our ears.

Congratulations! You have all passed through the lesser domain of Morpheus, managed by Epiales.

Time used: 10 Hours
Time Remaining: 2 Hours
Distance Travelled: 100 Kilometers

Challenge Complete!

Contribution:
Shawn Adams: 42%
Hudson Mitchell: 41%
Rebecca Harris: 12%
Anna Harris: 5%

Allocating Rewards.

Ha, I thought to myself, even after all that I still wasn't the highest contributor. How fun. I grimaced as I looked around at my allies. Mentally preparing myself for being whisked to the king's palace once more.

Once I reopened my eyes, we were all seated on chairs in an imposing marble hall. The king towered above us on his golden throne, his stern gaze weighing heavily upon each of us. His crown, a circlet of sharp, glimmering laurels, sat proudly on his brow, and his robes were embroidered with symbols of power and dominance. He was not just a ruler; he was a monument to kingship itself.

This was no ordinary trial. The air itself seemed to hum with tension, and an unshakable feeling of inevitability pressed down on me like a vice. The former King of Athens, Erikthonius, regarded us with a gaze sharp enough to cut steel.

"Congratulations," he began, his voice reverberating in the vast hall. "You are on trial. You were not meant to pass beyond thirty kilometers in the lesser realm of Morpheus."

His words were measured, deliberate, yet carried the weight of finality. "You defied the laws of his domain, and now you must answer for your transgressions."

A cold shiver ran down my spine. We were not just facing punishment; we were facing a ruler whose power stretched beyond the mortal coil, a king who had seen empires rise and fall. There was no sympathy in his eyes, only the expectation of obedience and explanation.

A potential patron is interested in this development.

That small notification floated in my vision, and it took every ounce of willpower not to react visibly. Someone was watching us, someone powerful enough to influence this trial. An Olympian? A god? Whoever it was, they were pulling strings in ways I couldn't yet fathom.

Fucking hell, I thought. *It's like every act of ours is being watched. Can I not even get a moment of peace?*

But no, there would be no peace here. If I showed weakness now, the consequences would be irreversible. I had to stay composed, had to think my way out of this.

The king's glare fell upon Anna first. She squirmed in her chair, her sister Rebecca gripping her hand tightly.

"How?" Erikthonius asked, his voice booming. "Explain to me how you managed to survive trekking through one of the domains of Morpheus?"

The curiosity from before was gone. This was interrogation, cold and cutting.

Anna cracked instantly. "We just followed Hudson!" she blurted out.

I closed my eyes briefly. *This bitch.* Throwing me under the bus without even a moment's hesitation. I glanced at Rebecca and Shawn, but they were frozen in fear.

The king's snarl reverberated through the hall. "Do not think I don't see through your schemes, woman." His words dripped with disdain, his piercing gaze making Anna shrink further into her seat. "However, you are right. And for now, I let it pass. Know this: if not for your potential patron," he spat the word like venom, ",I would have had you receive a fate worse than your sister for your lacking contribution."

Anna's face was pale with fear, but her eyes,those deceitful eyes,flickered with something else. Calculation? Defiance? Perhaps both.

The king then turned his focus to me, his gaze pinning me down like a butterfly on display.

"So, Hudson," he began, his voice a blade wrapped in silk. "You were the leader in their eyes. You made the call to take the leftmost path, the most dangerous route. And yet, here you all stand, alive. Tell me, mortal, why?"

My mind went blank. His eyes were suffocating, his aura oppressive. He *knew*. He somehow knew that I had been aware of the danger and chosen it anyway. I couldn't lie. Not to him. Not under *this* gaze.

"That's the thing, Your Majesty," I began weakly, my voice faltering. "I,I wasn't thinking,"

The king's roar interrupted me. "You *weren't thinking?!* Hilarious. Well, you can think now, can't you? Explain it to me, mortal. What went through your head?"

My throat was dry, and my chest felt tight. But something sparked in me, some ember of defiance.

"I wasn't thinking because I couldn't," I said. "I knew I couldn't match the wisdom of a goddess. I couldn't calculate the plans of someone so far above me. So I trusted my instincts."

The words hung heavy in the air. The king stared at me, his expression unreadable, his golden eyes fixed on mine.

"Interesting," he said at last, his voice softer but no less dangerous. "And what of the traps? The golden lights? How did you resist their pull?"

I hesitated, trying to form a plausible answer. But the king's gaze sharpened, and he leaned forward slightly.

"Cease your plotting, mortal," he said with quiet menace. "You cannot deceive me."

Then, like lightning, an idea struck me.

"A skill," I said confidently.

"Elaborate," the king commanded.

"I believe it was due to a skill I possess," I repeated, my smirk slipping out despite myself.

The king's nostrils flared. "Do not belittle me, mortal."

"Why are you feeling belittled, Your Majesty?" I asked, voice syrupy with false innocence. "I simply answered your question."

For a brief moment, the king seemed ready to unleash his wrath upon me. But before he could, a chime rang out in the air.

Your potential patron is proud and interfering.

It lasted less than a heartbeat, but I saw it, a flash of fear in the king's eyes. Fear. And then it was gone, replaced by the cold mask of royalty.

"Fine," the king said, straightening in his throne. "First and foremost, you are all *banned* from seeing your status until the end of the final challenge. You have two trials remaining. But Hudson,"

He leaned forward, his grin cruel.

"For the last trial, you will fight a beast. Alone."

My stomach sank.

"Now, as you know, the next challenge will be a viewing of your past, your trauma. What made you who you are. I will not see this trial, for it is something the system itself permits."

He leaned back, his final words heavy.

"I pray this makes you better people."

But I knew those words were aimed squarely at me. And I wasn't looking forward to this trial. Not one bit.

The king,his presence an oppressive weight in the air,gave us one last unreadable look before turning away, his heavy cloak trailing behind him as he disappeared into the shadows. His parting words echoed in my head like a death knell: *"Five minutes to prepare yourselves."*

Five minutes. Five measly minutes to brace for whatever fresh hell awaited us. Naturally, I had no time for such luxuries because, of course, Dumb and Dumber immediately descended upon me with all the subtlety of a wrecking ball.

"You *knew* it was the most dangerous?" Rebecca's voice was sharp, her eyes aflame with fury. "Are you insane?" She didn't even pause for breath before continuing. "No, scratch that,you *are* insane! Do you have any idea what you put us through?"

"Man," Shawn cut in, arms crossed over his broad chest, his brow furrowed in a way that suggested genuine confusion rather than anger. "Why the fuck did you antagonize the *former king of Athens*, bro? Nah, seriously, explain that shit."

"Wait a damn second, pudgy," Rebecca snapped her head toward Shawn briefly before focusing her glare back on me. "Don't you understand? This *fucker*",she jabbed an accusatory finger in my direction,"decided to put *all* of us in danger for shits and giggles. WHY?" She inhaled sharply, her face a furious shade of crimson. "No, better yet, HOW did you know?"

"You better have answers for us, Hudson," Shawn added, his voice low, but it carried weight.

I raised my hands in mock surrender. "Alright, alright! Fuck! Could you two back off for one goddamn second?"

Rebecca's glare intensified, and for a moment, I wondered if she might actually lunge at me. Her makeshift bandage, wrapped around the place where her hand used to be, was dark with dried blood. She noticed me glancing at it and let out a bitter laugh.

"Oh, don't even *start* with that pity look," she said, her voice trembling slightly despite the venom.

"Fine," I said, rubbing the back of my neck. "First,I don't know how to *explain* it, okay? I just... *knew.* I knew it was the most dangerous challenge, but I also *felt* like I could survive it. It was like... a gut feeling. So I wasn't scared."

Rebecca scoffed. "Oh, wonderful. A *gut feeling.* That makes it all better, doesn't it?"

"There you go with this whole 'I' thing,' Hudson," she continued, her voice dropping low, her words cutting like shards of glass. "'I knew.' 'I felt.' Did you ever,even for a *second*,think about *us*?"

She had me there. For all my bravado and faux confidence, she had me dead to rights. They were little more than flickering afterthoughts to me until we were all neck-deep in one of Morpheus' twisted domains.

I did what any self-respecting idiot would do: I ignored her accusation.

"Look, as you all know, we *did* survive," I said, trying to sound nonchalant. "And as for why I antagonized the former king... simple. It was fun."

Shawn blinked at me. Rebecca's mouth fell open.

"Yeah, yeah, I know," I continued hurriedly. "I have a bad habit, okay? I hate being looked down on. I can't stand it. And no, I will not elaborate further. But hey,I got my divine retribution, didn't I?" I gestured broadly at myself, trying to lighten the mood with an exaggerated grimace.

Silence.

Rebecca and Shawn exchanged glances, some unspoken agreement passing between them. Without another word, they turned and walked away, their shoulders tense, their expressions unreadable.

Good. That was over.

Except it wasn't.

Because then came Anna.

The oh-so-gentle healer, her every step calculated, her smile serene and unreadable. Where Rebecca was fire and Shawn was stone, Anna was ice,cool, quiet, and sharp enough to cut deep without leaving a mark.

"This is why I don't like being a leader," she said softly, almost as if she were speaking to herself. "So many naysayers. So many... *annoying* people."

Her voice was even, but there was a dangerous undercurrent beneath it,like a placid lake hiding razor-sharp rocks just below the surface.

Huh. That was... surprisingly honest. Interesting.

She sighed, brushing a strand of pale hair behind her ear. "But it's such a shame, isn't it? That I have to make myself known now."

Something clicked in my brain.

"Anna," I said, narrowing my eyes at her. "Why didn't you heal us throughout the last trial?"

Her smile widened slightly, but her eyes stayed cold.

"There wasn't a need," she said simply.

My stomach turned, and I had to remind myself,very firmly,who the most dangerous person in this group really was.

Oh, how I *wished* it was me.

Before I could respond, the air around us shimmered with a blinding flash of light, sharp and searing. I threw my arm up to shield my eyes, but it was too late. The world folded in on itself, and I felt myself being pulled,no, *wrenched*,into the void.

The next trial had begun.

Chapter 21. "Life can only be understood backwards; but it must be lived forwards." , Søren Kierkegaard

The world transformed, my eyes opened to that room, but this time with a 16-year-old me sitting in it. Was this how they felt, witnessing me? Someone who was still a child, broken, beaten,yet still with that look of defiance in my eyes. How poetic. Athena is really a devious bitch. She plotted this, surely, or at the very least wrote it in the code. How poetic indeed.

I knew it would be the room, with the same menacing torchlight, that only highlighted the blood on the floor. The walls, soggy with a putrid moss, loomed over me. Dammit, I still remember what I thought back then,the walls had eyes, and here I am, acting as those eyes. How fucking poetic. I knew this was the most traumatic part of my life, but I wondered,why did they show me this version? Barely a week into the torture, barely a week into the fear. I wasn't broken, not yet. I was scared for sure, but I didn't break. So that begged the question: what did they want to show me?

The boy sitting in that room,me,was so small. Smaller than I remember. His clothes hung loose, dirtied with grime and dried blood, a grotesque mosaic of suffering etched into every fiber. His face was hollow, sunken in from malnutrition and sleepless nights. And yet, there was fire in his eyes. A spark of something stubborn and untamed. It was strange, watching myself like this, as if I were both a spectator and an unwilling participant in the same tragedy.

I wanted to reach out, to tell him something,anything. That it would end, that he would make it out. But what could I say? What words could ever soothe a boy trapped in such a hell? The silence in the room felt alive, heavy, suffocating. Every flicker of the torch on the damp walls felt like a lash across my back, and every droplet of water dripping from the moss-covered ceiling sounded like the ticking of a bomb counting down.

How did I survive this? How did *he* survive this?

And yet, he did. I did. But survival isn't the same as living, is it? The boy in front of me wasn't just enduring physical agony; he was being reshaped, his mind broken apart and rearranged into something unrecognizable. I could almost hear his thoughts. The fear. The desperation. The fragile hope that clung to him despite everything.

But still, he sat there. Shoulders trembling but squared. His breathing is shallow but steady. His fists clenched so tightly that his knuckles turned white. Oh, how brave he was. How foolish. How tragic.

And by some wretched scheme, my question was answered with a scene shift. The boy within the room,me,was now on the verge of breaking. Oh, how poetic. They showed me how a man sat strongly; now they are showing me how weak and pathetic I was when I was on the verge.

The heartbreak I felt was absolutely agonizing. Why was I put through this? Was I targeted? Was I just some unlucky brat who thought the world revolved around him? What the actual fuck is this? How could I, a boy at 16 years old, be a victim to this? I wanted to laugh at the madness of it all. But I couldn't.

Why, why, why. Why did they have to show me this? Do they not know how long it took me to be okay with this? I didn't heal, absolutely not. I just ignored it, like all the other problems in my life. I could feel my heart slowing down. I could feel chains grabbing around my lungs, a pain that I never felt in my 21 years of living. A pain I never felt when fighting the chimera, a pain I didn't feel whilst in the realm of Morpheus. Oh, how painful is memory. How miserable it is.

And then, while I was still being headstrong, I witnessed the scene change once more. They finally showed it. A broken man. No,a broken child. I witnessed myself scream until I lost my voice. I witnessed myself cry until my tears turned red. I witnessed myself bleed from my eyes, wailing without sound escaping, until the blood stopped as well. I witnessed myself shake and convulse, till my body remained limp. And then came the sirens. Rescuing me from that hell. Ha, rescuing. What an overused word. I wasn't rescued, I wasn't saved. I still went through it all. I still… broke.

And then the scene finished, and the pain followed. Let me ask you all: have you ever felt pain? Not the pain of loss. Not the pain of injury. What I am going to do now is explain what true pain is. The pain I felt. Pain is… unrelenting, condescending. Pain is stomach-wrenching, muscle-clenching. Pain. Pain is the most evil thing I can explain. Pain comes when you least expect it, you bottle it down, hoping it dies while it is hidden under bravado and courage. But it never goes away. Pain latches onto you. It sees when you're asleep, it sees when you're awake. Waiting patiently like an apex predator waiting to pounce. And what can you do? Nothing. You try therapy, you try talking about it, but the pain prevents you from doing it. I had a therapist once. She went to therapy after talking to me. How fucked up am I? I sent my own therapist to therapy.

The pain took over me. I couldn't speak, I couldn't breathe, I couldn't scream. I was in and out of consciousness for what seemed like an eternity. But I knew it only lasted for a while. I am probably just exaggerating how long I was out of it. Yeah, you guys don't want to hear from a broken man, do you? Not at all. I'm boring you with the details. But I never felt like a victim before this day five years ago. Now I am facing it again. And I have no control over my own body.

Why, why, why. Why is this still affecting me? I am 21 years old, probably nearing level 100 now. Yet I am still feeling this. Why? Why the fuck is this happening to me? I wanted to scream. I wanted to shout. But I couldn't. Although the current expanse was endless, I felt claustrophobic. Then, as if by some divine miracle:

Your potential patron recognizes your pain.

I felt seen. I wasn't alone,not really. Even if it is someone I don't even know. This 'patron' of mine knew my pain, he recognized it, he understood it.

In that moment, the weight lessened,not gone, but lessened. It was like someone had reached into the depths of my soul, into the festering wound where all the rot had been allowed to grow unchecked, and they placed a hand there. A hand that said, *I know this. I see this. I feel this with you.*

But is recognition enough? Is being seen truly enough to heal something so deeply fractured? I don't know. Maybe it isn't. Maybe the scars will always ache, and the nightmares will always linger. Maybe I'll always carry this weight. But for now,for this brief moment,it feels like something shifted. Something small. Something fragile.

And maybe that's acceptable. Maybe that's enough. Because, for the first time in what feels like forever, I can breathe again.

Finally, with a breath of fresh air, I saw a question before my eyes.

How do you feel after this? (⅓)

Oh wow. Oh wow. So this is the trial. They wanted to break me with this trauma, and then have the audacity to ask me how I feel. Wow. I felt like shit. I felt like I was that 16-year-old boy all over again. Small. Helpless. Drowning in emotions I didn't have the words for back then and still don't have the words for now. Why do this to me? Why now? Why in this sterile, cold space where every breath feels monitored, every twitch analyzed? I felt like all my pride, courage, dignity,everything I had carefully stitched together over the years,had been unraveled in one sharp pull.

I felt seen through. No, not just seen. Exposed. Flayed open and laid bare for something, I don't even know what, to pick through my broken parts. I felt like I was a five-star meal of trauma and brokenness served on a silver platter, garnished with sprigs of barely concealed rage.

But that isn't what they want, I don't think. They don't want honesty, not really. They want some profound bullshit about how I grew through witnessing this. About how I emerged stronger, wiser, a shining beacon of resilience. But so what? So what if I'm supposed to sit here and perform emotional eloquence for them like some kind of trained seal?

No. I'm going to be honest.

I opened my mouth, and with a voice sharp as daggers, I said, "Like absolute shit. Give me the next question, you bitch."

Now, I know what you're thinking. It isn't a good idea to antagonize an almighty system, but you guys know how it is. A bad habit of mine. One I'll probably never change. So what? The words were out there now, sharp and irretrievable, and I was bracing myself for consequences that never came. Instead, a new question appeared before me.

If you were to tell your younger self one thing, what would it be and why?

The fuck is this? An English lecture? A TED Talk? Why are you asking me this as if there's some profound, life-altering answer waiting in the wings of my mind? The truth was,I didn't know. I had no idea what I would tell my younger self. What could I possibly say to him that would change anything? Is there anything I could tell him that would make the pain lessen? Probably not.

I knew how I was after that incident. I didn't care for anyone. I didn't accept help from a single soul. I trusted myself least of all. My mind was a prison, and every thought was another guard keeping me locked in. What could I say to him now that would make a difference? What words would reach him through the walls he had already started building? None, probably. But still, I tried to find something,anything,that might resonate.

And then an answer came to me. An answer that he would appreciate. It wasn't the full truth, but it wasn't a lie either.

"You will live through this and reach higher heights. It won't be easy, but it will be necessary. And it will get better. I wish you nothing but the best.
Remember,always trust yourself above all others. As for why I would tell myself this? There's nothing else I can say. Any explanation would hurt him. But at least he's seen."

I let the words hang in the air for a moment, their weight settling around me like a heavy coat. Surprisingly, they were accepted. No rejection, no snide remarks, no cruel reminders of inadequacy. Just... acceptance.

And then came the final question.

What will you do now?

Seriously? Seriously? After all of this,after dragging me through my worst memories, after peeling back the layers of scars and old wounds,you want to know *what I will do now*? As if I'm supposed to have some grand, cinematic plan ready to deliver with a bow on top?

Were these questions designed to force me into introspection? Was this whole process just one big exercise in emotional excavation? And now, at the end of it, you want me to offer you some neat little resolution? A promise? A direction? Ha. How hilarious.

There's nothing I *can* do, is there? I've accepted that this trauma is me. It isn't something I can scrub away or package into a tidy narrative. But I also know I can't bury it again. It would be pathetic,*I* would be pathetic,if I went back to old habits. But where does that leave me? Somewhere between acceptance and paralysis, I suppose.

I wish I could say I had some philosophically profound answer, but I didn't. The truth is, I didn't know what I would do. Not really. But I knew one thing: I couldn't let

181

this moment slip away without anchoring it to something real.

So I opened my mouth once more and simply stated, "I will remember this and not forget how I was at my weakest."

The words hung there, simple yet heavy. And for once, it felt like enough.

There was no applause, no grand revelation, no triumphant music swelling in the background. Just silence. The kind of silence that feels like both an ending and a beginning.

And maybe that was the point.

It was at this point i got my grade

Trial Complete
Level of Trauma A⁻
Level of Response B
Rewards Allocated

The realization hit me hard,my trauma wasn't even the worst. Grade A-, they said, like it was some sort of consolation prize. "Not even that bad," I muttered to myself, the words cutting deeper every time I thought of them. Yet here I am, broken, struggling to function, stuck in a spiral of shame. How pathetic is that? To feel so utterly wrecked by something that, apparently, isn't even the worst? The weight of it all crushed me, and I hated myself for letting it. I wanted to scream, to claw my way out of this pit, but instead, I sat there, choking on the idea that my pain was somehow less valid.

What stung even more was the thought that I wasn't unique. I had always believed no one could truly understand what I'd been through, that my pain was too big, too personal for anyone else to grasp. But now I'm being told that others have it worse, that I'm just a small fish in a vast ocean of suffering. It made me feel insignificant, like my struggles didn't matter. The shame twisted into anger,at myself for being so weak and at the whole concept of measuring pain. But beneath the anger was fear, a nagging voice that whispered maybe they're right, maybe I really am just not strong enough. And that thought, more than anything, left me drowning.

Whilst I was struggling with my emotions, I felt the familiar feeling rush through my blood. A sign that I was about to present myself to the king once again.

Chapter 22. "Our life is frittered away by detail... Simplify, simplify." , Henry David Thoreau

As my eyes opened in the familiar throne room, the sheer grandeur of the space seemed to mock the turmoil churning within me. The beautiful pillars now loomed around us shimmering faintly under the golden light that emanated from an unseen source. The king's throne, a massive construct of gleaming black stone and gold filigree, sat atop a raised dais at the far end, exuding a dominance that could silence even the most rebellious of spirits. I looked around at my companions, noting their expressions as we all processed the traumas we had just endured. Each face told its own story,each one a testament to the cruelty of this system.

Shawn, ever the simpleton, wore an incredulous smile. It was as if he'd found some semblance of closure, some twisted solace in the horrors he'd faced. How quaint. How utterly naïve. He seemed almost giddy, his hands fidgeting with nervous energy. I wanted to despise him for it, for the audacity of finding comfort where I found none. But I couldn't. Who was I to judge? Here I was, holding myself above the rest, only for the system to drag me down from that imagined pedestal, forcing me to confront the fragility of my own existence.

Then there was the fallen archer. She looked the worst of all, her usual fierce demeanor replaced by an unsettling vulnerability. Her hands trembled as she gripped her bow, knuckles white with the force of her grip. Her eyes, usually sharp and alert, seemed haunted, darting around the room as if expecting an unseen assailant. Whatever she'd experienced, it had left her hollow. And yet, I couldn't shake the nagging feeling that her trauma paled in comparison to Anna's.

Anna,the healer, the cold and calculating one,was a shell of her former self. She wore the same blank expression I did, her face devoid of any emotion, but her eyes betrayed her. Those eyes, once so filled with cunning, now held a hollow, defeated look. The spark of intelligence, the sharpness that had always been her hallmark, was gone. She was a mirror of my own despair, holding herself together out of sheer necessity. She composed herself as best she could, standing straight and stoic, waiting for the king's next decree.

And then there was the king.

He sat upon his throne with an ease that spoke of absolute authority. In his hand, he held a parchment, which he regarded with a faint, almost amused smile. The king's presence was suffocating. He didn't need to posture or demand respect; it was woven into the very fabric of his being. He was the arbiter, the architect of our torment, and he reveled in the power he wielded over us. His role as our guide had long since lost its novelty for him. Now, it seemed, we were merely pawns in his game, a source of mild amusement to break the monotony of his eternal rule.

"Well, isn't this interesting," he began, his voice echoing through the cavernous hall. "One C grade, one B grade, and two A grades." He looked down at us, his piercing gaze scanning for any sign of reaction. His words hung in the air like a sword poised to strike. Of course, he knew everything. Hoping otherwise would have been foolish.

He continued, his tone measured but tinged with condescension. "While I know not the details of your traumas, I have a gauge of how harrowing they must have been. And I am impressed that the two with the highest level faced the worst. Not that it is surprising,merely unexpected."

The king's words were a trap, a lure designed to provoke a response, but none of us took the bait. The silence that followed was palpable, broken only by the faint hum of magic that permeated the room. For a fleeting moment, his mask slipped, revealing a flash of irritation. But it was gone just as quickly, replaced by a sly, cunning smile that sent a chill down my spine.

"Now, I will tell you all of the next task," he announced, leaning forward slightly. "As you all know, Mister A Grade will have to challenge a beast on his own." He gestured toward me, and I felt the weight of the room shift toward me. I braced myself against the oppressive atmosphere, unwilling to show any outward sign of weakness.

"Now, what you don't know," the king continued, his grin widening, "is that in order to punish the outlier, we had to lower the level of the beast the three of you will face. It will still be difficult, of course, but not impossible. As for you, Hudson, you will face a beast of similar level,alone."

The king's eyes locked onto mine, gleaming with sadistic delight. He was savoring this moment, imagining my defeat, my humiliation, perhaps even my death. My throat tightened, but I forced myself to hold my ground. Showing weakness now would only feed his contempt.

"Do you have any questions?" the king asked, his voice dripping with mockery. He knew as well as we did that no answer would alleviate the dread hanging over us. Still, he waited, reveling in the power he held over us.

I spoke first, my voice laced with barely contained venom. "How long is left in the tutorial?"

The king chuckled, clearly amused by my defiance. "Oh, Hudson," he said, his tone mocking. "Are you not going to show your superior any respect?" But he answered my question regardless. "The tutorial will end tomorrow. Some of you will leave with permission to meet your potential patron. Some of you won't."

Tomorrow. The word echoed in my mind like a promise and a curse. One more day in this accursed labyrinth. One more day of enduring this nightmare. I clenched my fists, forcing myself to focus on that glimmer of an endpoint.

Anna was the next to speak, her voice steady but tinged with a faint tremor. "Your majesty, what is the beast we are to fight?"

The king's gaze shifted to her, and for a moment, his expression softened. "See, Hudson," he said, looking back at me, "that is how you show respect." His tone was cutting, designed to belittle, but I met his gaze unflinchingly. He scoffed before continuing. "Originally, the design was for you all to face one of Arachne's children. Yet, due to a certain someone",he glanced at me pointedly,"that has been changed. The group of three will face a small flock of Stymphalian birds, whereas the troublemaker will face three Empousa."

Anna bowed her head in gratitude, murmuring a soft "Thank you, your majesty." The king's gaze swept over us once more, his expression unreadable.

"You have ten minutes to collect yourselves and prepare for the battle ahead," he declared, his tone final. With that, he leaned back into his throne, his attention seemingly elsewhere, as if we were already forgotten.

The countdown has begun, and the weight of the impending battle settled over us like a shroud. Ten minutes. Just ten minutes to steel ourselves against the horrors yet to come.

"Hudson, are you alright?" Shawn's voice was soft, tinged with genuine concern that grated on me more than I cared to admit. He pitied me, and that was something I could never stomach. Being seen as broken, fragile,it was unbearable. I could tell he meant well; that he was just being kind. But kindness like his only served to remind me of how far I'd fallen.

"Nah, don't worry, mate. I've lowkey gotten over the trauma," I replied, forcing a smile that I hoped looked convincing. The truth, though, was far messier. I wasn't sure I had "gotten over" anything. Facing the trauma had helped, ironically enough, but not in the way one might think. I hadn't accepted it, hadn't healed from it. I had simply decided I could never allow myself to reach that breaking point again. Ever.

Shawn chuckled, clearly relieved. "Hey, at least that's something, man." He gave me a nudge on the shoulder, his easy grin lighting up his face. "What about the Empo... Empa... whatchamacallit?"

His butchered pronunciation cracked me up. I let out a genuine laugh, the first in what felt like ages. "If you're talking about the Empousa, I just have to take it headfirst," I said, my voice steadier now.

"Good plan," Shawn said with a grin. "Just make sure it doesn't eat your face or something. I don't think they make prosthetics for that."

Before I could respond, Rebecca's sharp voice cut through the air. "You know, I'm still not over you leading us into danger, Mister A-Grade."

Her words dripped with disdain, and I turned to meet her glare. It wasn't the first time she'd taken a jab at me, but there was something different in her tone this time,a bitterness that ran deeper than usual.

"Hey, we lived, didn't we, Miss C-Grade?" I shot back with a smirk, feeling the corners of my mouth tug upward despite myself. I wasn't in the mood to argue, but Rebecca had a way of pulling me out of my thoughts, whether I liked it or not.

Her eyes narrowed. "Shut up, asshole. You get what you deserve."

"Aww, are you thankful that I lowered the level for you?" I teased, leaning back with a grin. I was having too much fun, I admit. There was nothing quite like getting under Rebecca's skin,especially since she took everything so personally.

Rebecca huffed and turned her attention back to Shawn, who was now attempting to mediate between us with his usual lighthearted humor. Their voices faded into the background as I noticed the healer,Anna,taking a seat beside me.

She folded her arms and tilted her head, her piercing gaze studying me. "So, do you want to share with a fellow A-Grade?"

"Not particularly. You?" I asked, throwing her question back at her. She shook her head, a wry smile tugging at her lips.

"Nope. Just thought I'd ask," she replied.

For a moment, we sat in silence, a rare pause in the chaos. Then Anna broke it. "So, are you prepared to meet your new potential patron?"

My brows shot up. "So you knew? Let me guess,I'm not the only one with a special new patron," I said, chuckling. Anna's smirk deepened, and she nodded slowly, clearly enjoying my reaction.

"You're not wrong," she said cryptically.

There was something calculating in her expression now, the kind of look that reminded me why I didn't fully trust her. She was sharp, strategic,a survivor, no doubt,but there was something crooked about her that set me on edge.

"Any advice?" I asked, half-joking.

She shrugged. "Don't die." Her smirk widened as she leaned in. "Seriously, though. I hope you get someone powerful as your first patron. Don't make this boring, Hudson."

"Noted," I replied dryly.

Her eyes gleamed with something unreadable as she continued. "You know, I don't want to see any of you three after this tutorial."

Her words caught me off guard, but I quickly recovered. "What, not even your own twin?" I asked, raising an eyebrow.

For a brief moment, her face darkened, shadows flickering behind her eyes. But then her expression shifted, and a grin spread across her lips, a grin that sent a chill down my spine. "She's a liability," Anna said cheerfully, her tone oozing with twisted glee. "And more importantly, she's not someone I care for."

I stared at her, trying to process what she'd just said. There was no trace of remorse in her voice, only cold detachment.

"Right," I muttered, unsure of what else to say.

"Anyway," Anna said, standing up and brushing off her hands, "don't screw this up, Hudson. I'll be watching." With that, she disappeared into the crowd, leaving me alone with my thoughts.

The others had drifted off too, each preoccupied with their own worries and preparations. I closed my eyes and took a deep breath, trying to steady my nerves. The Empousa awaited, and there was no room for hesitation. Not anymore.

As I stood there, I replayed the interactions in my mind, Shawn's kindness, Rebecca's bitterness, Anna's cold detachment. Each of them had their own struggles, their own battles to fight. And so did I.

"Time to finish this," I whispered to myself, stepping forward into the unknown.

Chapter 22. "Invisible threads are the strongest ties." , Friedrich Nietzsche.

Shawns Pov.

Birds. That was our task, apparently. I don't get it,what could make birds so dangerous? I mean, in this world, anything can be dangerous, but honestly, why is there a bird that sounds so much like an infection? From now on, I'm calling them staph birds. I'm not even going to bother pronouncing it properly, not after embarrassing myself in front of Hudson. Ugh, what a pain. And to top it off, we're now missing a certain six-foot soldier who's somehow more monstrous than the monsters we're facing.

Yeah, that's probably the best way to describe Hudson. He's a soldier,and a damn good one. And trust me, I know soldiers. I'm a midshipman in the navy, after all, though I doubt anyone cares about ranks or experience here. This world has a funny way of making all that irrelevant. Honestly, I knew this new world would break us the moment we arrived. I was purposefully rude to test everyone, to see who'd crack. Hudson? He's the type who would've been kicked out of the navy without so much as a warning. The guy loves to kill,he's mentally ill, I swear. But in this world? In this world, he's a godsend. Behind his madness, there's a method. He has a natural talent for slaughter, almost as if this place was designed for him.

But now, we're missing the talent of an unappreciated genius. Instead, I'm stuck with a pair of twins, inseparable to an insufferable degree. Rebecca's a natural sniper and tracker, but she lacks patience. She's headstrong, always pushing back against authority. She'd have been kicked out of the navy too, but unlike Hudson, she would've at least been warned first. Her missing arm? That's no one's fault but her own. It's infuriating. Not only am I missing our scarred prodigy, but I'm stuck with a cripple,and her sister.

Anna, though, is different. Quiet. Quaint. Cute, even. She reminds me of my daughter. She doesn't belong in this world, not at all. She probably had her whole life ahead of her before getting stuck here. Monsters don't belong in her story,especially not the kind that hunts us. She's too quiet, too innocent. Honestly, I'm just thankful she's still alive. But something doesn't sit right with me. In our last challenge, we had two A-grade traumas. Hudson, obviously, was one of them. But Anna? How does someone so bright carry a trauma of the same grade? I wish I could figure it out.

That wish was granted, without warning.

"From now on, I'm taking the lead," Anna proclaimed, her voice steady, unwavering. "I'm going to make myself known. I need you to survive because I can't hit as hard as the rest of you." She mumbled something else under her breath, but strangely, I didn't care. Whether it was curiosity or reluctance, I wanted to listen. I wanted to give her a chance. There was something in her eyes,a glint, no, a glow.

It was as if, for the first time, Anna wasn't just surviving. She was about to thrive.

"A flock of Stymphalian birds. That is what we are facing. Most known in the twelve labors of Heracles. The young hero had to get rid of a much bigger flock with loud noises. But we are not as strong as him, nor are we simply driving them away. We are hunting them." She looked at us, waiting for us to answer, and naturally, as the socialite I am, I responded.

"What do you want us to do?" I asked with a smile on my face. It was as if I was watching my own daughter grow up before me. I probably looked too proud of myself for asking what was honestly a very simple question.

She looked toward me with a look of accomplishment. "First, we need to scout out the size of the flock. The best person for this will be you, Bex," she told her former archer sister.

Rebecca looked up with woe in her eyes. "But how? How am I meant to do this, sis? I lost my arm, for fuck's sake." She pointed at her nub with bitter hatred, perhaps realizing that she lost her arm due to her own mistake.

Anna looked down at her sister with a smile on her face, as if she expected this very question to be asked. "Oh, come on, Bex. You were shortlisted by the Greek goddess of the hunt; that has to mean something. And even though you lost your arm, you are not useless. Tell me, have you ever heard of the legend of Celtic mythology Nuada Airgetlám?" She paused for a moment, gauging reactions before continuing. "He was a fierce king who lost his arm in battle and later used a prosthetic to continue to shoot. But the prosthetic was forged from silver. Are you telling me that in the middle of war you truly think he was just twiddling his thumbs waiting for the arm? No, I don't think so. He must have continued to fight for his people, with only one arm. Now I'm asking you to do the same for me," she told Rebecca empathetically. My thoughts, however, were different. How in the hell did Anna have knowledge of Celtic mythology? Greek I can understand; Norse, maybe; Egyptian, sure. But Celtic? Who knew she would be more knowledgeable on mythology than Hudson?

"I need you to scout it out, nothing more. Just figure out how big the flock is and then report back to us. You're the fastest,we need you." She continued her commands. "Shawn, you're our heavy hitter. Depending on what Rebecca tells us, you'll deal most of the damage. You will hold the fort." It was at this point that I realized I had underestimated the healer. She was a true strategist, someone we could rely on.

Without another word, Rebecca darted off to scout our prey, Anna reminding her to use a vantage point far enough away not to be noticed and yet high enough to see the entirety of the flock. Anna then turned her attention to me, and for a moment, I felt both secure and fearful,a strange echo of how I felt about the missing swordsman.

While Rebecca was away, Anna was fiddling with what seemed to be twine and beckoned me closer. I must admit, I was curious, though I tried to mask it by acting overly eager.

"What's up, Anna? What are you doing?" I asked, trying to sound calm but coming across a bit too enthusiastic.

"I'm creating a trap," she said nonchalantly, as if it should be obvious. She sighed and continued. "We have no idea how large the flock of birds will be until my sister returns. Regardless, we will need a way to slay all the birds at once. The deities might become restless and put another time limit on us. I would rather not have a repeat of the last round."

I nodded slightly, her remark reminding me of the horror of Morpheus's lesser realm as well as my own failure. I wasn't great at planning; honestly, I never had to be. But I needed to learn, and fast.

"So, what do you want me to do?" I asked, probably a little too quickly, like a student eager to answer the wrong question in class. I realized I was fidgeting and forced myself to stand still, which probably made me look even more awkward.

"Well, I don't want you to help with the net, so why don't you tell me what you can do?" she responded in a somewhat mocking way, but her tone told me something different. She was curious, evaluating me, testing me. I needed to think this through.

I'm not a strategist. The only reason I got my rank was due to my loyalty to my country and my determination. So how am I to answer this? I needed to prove that I was useful. I thought back to the only book I'd read in recent years,the one my tentmate had shared with me from time to time. I thought about all the myths I learned. This is Athena's trial, so a Greek myth would be for the best. Then I thought of Hephaestus's trap. He captured the god of war and the goddess of love in a net, right? But they should have been able to escape easily if it were normal. I didn't have the material to make a powerful net, but Anna was already making one. How could I prevent any escape?

Then it hit me. Insect traps. On tour, we had to deal with damned insects, and the traps always worked because they were sticky. That's what we needed,something sticky.

Finally, I spoke. "I'll find something sticky to put on the net." I looked at Anna, hoping she knew what could work.

She nodded, her face lighting up. "Sap. Find sap from the trees and spread it on the net."

Without hesitation, I went off, gathering all the sap I could find. By the time I returned, Rebecca had also come back, her face grim but determined.

Chapter 24. "Every battle is won before it is fought." , Sun Tzu.

Rebecca glances at me, beckoning me to sit by the twins near the flickering flames of the campfire. Her sharp eyes drift down to my hands, which are still covered in sticky, golden sap. Her expression twists into something between disbelief and exasperation.

"Why were you playing with sap?" she asks incredulously, her voice carrying a slight edge.

"We are making a net to trap the birds, and I thought we might need something sticky," I responded, a bit defensively. My explanation earns a brief nod of approval from her, though her eyes still linger on my hands, clearly unconvinced of my brilliance.

She brushes past it and begins recounting her earlier reconnaissance. "Twenty. Twenty birds. The flock isn't as bad as I thought. The birds are quite big, though, about the size of vultures. Thankfully, they're slow. I can outrun them. Don't think you two can, though."

Anna, the quieter twin, tilts her head back to gaze at the sky, her lips pursed in thought. It's easy to imagine the gears turning in her head, formulating one of her meticulously detailed plans. There's a lull in the conversation, the kind of silence that feels awkward and heavy. I decide that maybe it's my duty to break it, but before I can blurt out something,anything,Anna speaks.

"Alright. First things first," she says with a commanding tone, gesturing toward a massive net laid out beside her. "I made the net. It should be large enough."

I glance at the net, and to my surprise, it's enormous. The thing could easily hold all the birds with room to spare. My earlier contribution suddenly feels embarrassingly unnecessary. Sap, really? Who was I kidding?

"Unfortunately," Anna continues, "I overestimated how large the flock would be. That means the sap is necessary, Shawn. We can't let them get loose, after all."

"Oh," I mutter. "That's... unfortunate." I'm not sure what else to say. My genius idea is reduced to an afterthought, and now I'm stuck as the guy who "helped" with sap. Still, I nod dutifully. Best to trust the strategist here.

Anna's gaze shifts to Rebecca. "Bex, you need to attract their attention. Be loud, be annoying, get them to chase you, then lead them to the net."

Rebecca squints at her sister. "Um, Anna, what if... what if they're scared of sounds instead?"

For a moment, Anna's face hardens. Her jaw tightens, her brow furrows, and she looks at Rebecca like she just suggested befriending the birds instead of catching them. The tension is palpable, and I'm not sure if I should step in or stay silent.

"So you're telling me," Anna says slowly, her voice dripping with irritation, "you didn't even check if the birds were scared of noises?"

Rebecca shrinks slightly under Anna's glare, scratching absently at the stump where her arm used to be. "I-I didn't think about it," she admits, her voice barely above a whisper.

Anna exhales sharply, her frustration evident. "Haah. Never mind. If they're scared of noises, then use the noise to drive them toward us. Is everyone clear on the plan?"

Rebecca and I nod, though I'm not entirely convinced of my own competence at this point. Anna seems to notice but doesn't comment.

"Good. Now we need to sleep. We'll commence the plan at midday tomorrow." Without another word, she turns and strides into her tent, Rebecca following close behind.

Left alone by the fire, I stare at the flickering flames, trying not to overthink everything. Did I really think sap would be revolutionary? I shake my head and crawl into my tent, muttering a silent prayer that tomorrow goes well.

I was jolted awake by a deafening noise, a sound so piercing it seemed to shake the very fabric of my dreams. Startled, I scrambled to sit upright, my heart pounding like a war drum. It took a moment for me to remember where I was,inside my modest tent, nestled amidst the wilderness we'd been traversing for weeks.

Still half-asleep, I fumbled with the tent flap and poked my head outside. Standing there, with a grin that stretched ear to ear, was Rebecca, the group's ever-enthusiastic archer. Her face was alight with a mixture of mischief and pride.

"Damn," she began, her voice loud enough to rival the noise that had woken me. "That was louder than I expected!" She chuckled, brushing a stray strand of hair from her face. "If it worked on you, the guy who sleeps through just about anything, it'll definitely scare off some birds."

Before I could muster a coherent response,or scold her for the assault on my ears,she turned on her heel and marched off, presumably to test her trap on the actual birds.

I groaned, rubbing my temples as the ringing in my ears persisted. The noise had been bad enough to disorient me, and I stumbled out of the tent, feeling as though the ground beneath me was swaying. My balance was off, my senses dulled. Was it really necessary for me to be her unwitting test subject?

Grumbling under my breath, I made my way to where Anna was working. I had a question burning in my mind, one that had been gnawing at me for weeks now. It wasn't just the noise or the exhaustion that had been weighing on me. No, it was something deeper,an ache in my soul, a nagging sense of inadequacy that refused to be ignored.

The truth was, I felt useless.

From the mole rat incident to the chimera attack, and even the labyrinth trial, every chance I'd had to prove myself seemed to slip through my fingers. Each time, someone else rose to the occasion, outshining me in every conceivable way. Hudson, with his unshakable confidence and raw skill, always gave me opportunities to step into the spotlight. But Anna… Anna made me feel like I was just *there*. A bystander. Maybe she didn't mean to, but her actions often left me questioning my worth.

The only thing I had going for me was my strength and my ability to endure. That was it. I was the shield, the brute force, the last line of defense. But deep down, I wanted to be more. I wanted to *matter*.

As I staggered to where Anna was setting up her trap, I steeled myself. I couldn't let this self-doubt consume me. If I wanted answers, I had to ask. Even if the question made me seem vulnerable or desperate, it was better than remaining silent.

When I found Anna, she was crouched near a pair of towering trees, her hands deftly tying knots in a nearly invisible net. The trap was a masterpiece of ingenuity,cleverly camouflaged, yet undeniably effective. The glisten of my sap on the net confirmed that my contribution hadn't been entirely useless. At least I'd helped with *something*.

"Hey, Anna. How are you?" I asked, trying to sound casual. My voice betrayed me, though, cracking slightly under the weight of my nerves.

She didn't look up, her focus entirely on her work. "I'm preparing the trap, as you can see," she replied, gesturing to the intricate setup before her.

This was it. I couldn't hold back any longer. I took a deep breath, willing my voice to stay steady. "Listen, I was wondering… what do I have to do? What's my role in all this?"

She paused, her hands freezing mid-knot. For a moment, I thought I'd offended her. Then she muttered something under her breath before turning to face me with a sweet, reassuring smile.

"Oh, Shawn, you are the most pivotal person in this plan," she said, her tone warm and sincere.

Her words caught me off guard. "I am?" I asked, blinking in disbelief. How could that be true?

"Yes, you are," she continued, her voice brimming with conviction. "We need your strength. Once the birds are trapped, we can't afford to waste any time. We need power,raw, unrelenting power,to finish them off as quickly as possible. And that's where you come in.

You're the one who can do it, Shawn. Kill as many as you can for me."

Her confidence in me was almost overwhelming. For the first time in what felt like forever, I felt seen. Appreciated. Anna wasn't so different from Hudson after all,kind, supportive, and willing to trust me with an important task.

But as her words sank in, so did the weight of my responsibility. I glanced at my greatsword, its blade gleaming faintly in the sunlight. Could I really do it? Could I single handedly cut through a flock of Stymphalian birds? A hammer would've been better suited for the job, but I didn't have that luxury. All I had was my sword and the strength I'd been honing for years.

As I stood there, grappling with my doubts, a notification flashed before my eyes:

A deity is interested in your plight.

The message was cryptic, but its timing was uncanny. Was this some kind of sign? An acknowledgment of my struggles? If even a deity recognized my turmoil, maybe I wasn't imagining things. Maybe I really had been falling short. The thought weighed on me like a crushing burden, but it also sparked a flicker of hope.

Perhaps this deity,whoever they were,could guide me. Perhaps they saw something in me that I couldn't see in myself.

Before I could dwell on it any further, Anna called out to me, snapping me back to reality. She instructed me to hide behind one of the trees, ready to strike when the time came. I obeyed, positioning myself out of sight but within striking distance of the net.

Moments later, a familiar deafening noise filled the air. I turned toward the source and saw Rebecca sprinting toward the trap, banging on her chestplate with her one good arm. She was grinning wildly, clearly enjoying the chaos she was creating.

Behind her, the flock of Stymphalian birds surged forward like a living storm. Their wings beat the air with a thunderous rhythm, and their shrill cries added to the cacophony. They moved as one, a chaotic mass of feathers and fury, their beady eyes locked on Rebecca.

She pushed herself to the limit, her breaths coming in ragged gasps as she neared the net. Ten meters. Five. One. At the last possible moment, she dove out of the way, rolling to safety as the birds barreled straight into the trap.

The net snapped shut around them, ensnaring the entire flock in a writhing, screeching mass. They thrashed and clawed at their bonds, but the more they struggled, the tighter the net became.

This was my moment.

I stepped out from behind the tree, gripping my greatsword with both hands. My muscles tensed as I raised the blade high above my head, my body coiling like a bowstring. Pain shot through me,sharp and searing,but I didn't let it stop me.

With a primal roar, I unleashed all my strength in a single, devastating strike. The blade came crashing down, its impact resonating like a thunderclap. The ground beneath me trembled, and a shockwave rippled outward, silencing the cries of the trapped birds.

The aftermath was a blur. My body screamed in protest, every muscle cramping as the backlash of my attack hit me like a tidal wave. Anna rushed to my side, her hands glowing with healing magic as she worked to ease my pain.

"Are they… are they all dead?" I managed to ask through gritted teeth.

She nodded, her eyes filled with a mixture of relief and admiration. "You did it, Shawn. They're all gone."

A new notification appeared before me:

Trial Complete.
22 Stymphalian Birds Slain.

Contribution:
Anna Harris: 35%
Shawn Alexander Adams: 34%
Rebecca Harris: 31%

Allocating Rewards…

New Skill Unlocked:
One Smash:
The user channels every ounce of their strength, energy, and resolve into a devastating downward strike that delivers unmatched destructive power. This single, focused attack unleashes a shockwave that shakes the ground and obliterates anything within its impact radius. However, the immense strain of executing this move leaves the user paralyzed for 5 seconds, rendering them vulnerable.

A sense of pride welled up within me. I'd done it. I'd not only proven my worth but also unlocked a new skill,a skill that embodied everything I'd been striving for.

As the trial's magic whisked us away to the throne room, I couldn't help but wonder what awaited us next. Hudson was already there, laughing with the king like old friends. What had he faced in his solo trial? What had he learned?

Whatever lay ahead, I knew one thing for certain: I wasn't useless. Not anymore.

Chapter 25. "If you are lonely when you're alone, you are in bad company." , Plato.

Hudson POV:

I wondered how the king was going to push me. I knew it would be difficult, impossible even. It would be irrational for me to assume otherwise. So as I stepped into this new space, the first thing I noticed was the silence. It wasn't just quiet; it was eerily so, like the world had taken a deep breath and forgotten to exhale. The corridor stretched out before me, long and dim, its walls scrutinizing my every movement, every hesitation. I was being watched. Judged.

Then I saw it, something that stood out against the oppressive darkness. A light.

A light at the end of the tunnel. What a cliché. A final joke played at my expense. It beckoned me forward, pulling me towards it, towards my fate, towards my demise. And as much as I wished I could turn away, my feet had no choice but to move. I stepped forward, a prisoner of destiny, marching to the beat of an unseen drum.

With each step, the light grew. So did the noise.

A low hum at first, like an irritating whisper in my ear. But then it grew, an incessant, buzzing cacophony. It felt as if the universe itself was mocking me. Each step I took made it louder, a jeering chorus that grated against my bones. But despite the aggravation, despite the insult to my circumstance, I didn't stop. I couldn't. The moment I hesitated, I was dead.

Then the buzzing changed. No longer a jeer, but something else. Louder. Rhythmic.

Cheers.

That's when I understood. That's when I realized the true setting of this trial. This was an arena. The light wasn't just an exit, it was a doorway. A doorway to my battle. To my opponents. To my prey.

And of course, they thought the same of me.

The moment I stepped into the blinding brightness, the crowd erupted, screaming my name louder than any bloodthirsty deity. Why? I didn't know. I didn't care. My body trembled with anticipation, not from fear, but from something far greater. Was this it? Was this my grand recognition? Were all my misfortunes finally worth something?

I stepped further, my eyes adjusting, and there they were. My adversaries. My executioners.

Three of them stood at the opposite end of the arena, their forms dripping with seductiveness. Beautiful in a way that felt artificial, like a perfectly sculpted painting hiding something grotesque beneath its surface. Their lips curled into smiles, but their eyes... their eyes betrayed them. Slitted pupils like those of reptiles, claws twitching with hunger, wings drawn back, poised for battle.

They didn't try to hide their bloodlust. No pretense. No illusions.

This would be a fight to the death.

I activated my Identify skill, bracing myself for the reality of my situation. The information flashed before me.

3x Empousa (D)
HP: 25000 x 3

And then another notification. A message.

Your potential patron warns you of danger.

A warning? A futile gesture. I already knew. This is the wall that was impossible for any mortal to surpass in the tutorial. The king had sent me here to die. The cheers were not a celebration, but a farewell hymn. The final song before my death.

I was nothing but a feast served on a silver platter.

But I wasn't going to let them eat.

I gritted my teeth and focused. I couldn't lose myself in my own madness, not again. The last time I let go, I had nearly crossed a point of no return. If I lost myself here, it was over.

My instincts sharpened. My eyes locked onto the Empousai. My prey.

The first attacked without hesitation, wings flaring as she propelled forward, releasing a gust of wind. Sand flew into my eyes, burning, stinging, forcing me to drop to one knee. A perfect opening. She lunged for my neck.

But my eyes never closed.

With sheer will, I raised my sword, steel meeting talons in a screeching clash. The force of the blow sent her skidding back. Her arrogance had cost her. I surged forward, blade seeking flesh, aiming for a killing strike.

Then the second struck.

Pain.

A deep gash tore across my side. Hot blood spilled, staining the sand beneath me. I swung wildly, desperate to retaliate, to take a head, to claim a victory.

But my arms. They were weak. My strength was leaving me. My vision blurred. My body begged for surrender.

And yet. They were getting slower. My instincts weren't wrong. My logic was sound. If I kept calm, I could survive. If I let go, if I succumbed to the rage clawing at my mind, I would lose. My mind had to be sharper than my blade.

The battle devolved into a storm of steel and talons. Every strike drew blood,mine and theirs. Every breath came with fire, with agony. But I was smiling. I was winning. I could feel it.

Then, they smiled too.

Why? Were they enjoying this as much as I was? It didn't matter. All that meant was that we were both the same. We both loved the smell of blood. Loved the act of violence. That is what is important to us. And unfortunately for them only one of us would continue this.

I tried to lift my sword for one final strike. To finish it now. After all, all good things must come to an end.

But my sword didn't rise. Why? There was no poison. I would have been notified. This is something else. What did I miss? My patron warned me but why? The Empousa had another ability didn't they? What was it? I didn't have the time to read about it. What can I possibly do?

Then the cheers of the crowd blurred into white noise. The faces of the Empousai twisted into grins,mocking, triumphant. I had played their game, danced to their rhythm. And now, I was theirs.

I had thought I was the predator.

But I was always the prey.

Chapter 26. "A man can do what he wants, but not want what he wants." , Arthur Schopenhauer

It was at that point that I understood what I had missed. The Empousai were not combatants. At least, not really. They were masters of illusion, of deception, of weaving magic so subtle and intricate that reality itself bent to their whim. This arena was their playground, and I was a mere toy. The cheers that had once thundered in my ears, roaring like a symphony of triumph, now faded into nothingness,a white noise devoured by the abyss.

I stood alone in a barren coliseum, the crowd vanishing like dust in the wind. Athena and her child sneered down at me from above, their very presence mocking me. Moments ago, I had felt like a king, standing on the precipice of victory. But now? Now, I realized I had been nothing more than a fool dancing on the strings of a cruel marionette. How pathetic. How utterly, disgustingly pathetic.

Why had I believed, even for a second, that this trial would be simple? That my punishment would be light? That I, in my arrogance, could stride into this arena and emerge unscathed? It had barely been ten minutes, and yet I had deluded myself into thinking I could conquer something beyond my understanding.

My sword felt heavy, heavier than it ever had before. My body felt leaden, my will crumbling beneath the weight of my own hubris. I tried to reason, to strategize, to think my way out of this trap, but logic held no power here. I looked at the Empousa,not a single scratch marked their bodies. They had broken me without lifting a finger. Their smiles were knives, and I was on the verge of shattering.

They had wanted this. They had planned for this.

From the moment my personal trauma had been exposed, they had whispered it back to me, carving it into my mind with every trial, every illusion, every failure.

Damn that goddess. Damn her wisdom, damn her cruelty, damn her sadistic amusement. How dare she treat my fate as if it were a plaything? She was no Moirai, no weaver of destiny. She was a strategist, and I was merely another piece in her grand game.

I clenched my jaw, forcing myself to look once more at the Empousai, and that was when I noticed it.

Hope.

Their breathing was ragged. Their movements were sluggish. They had made a mistake. An illusion of this magnitude, one powerful enough to fool me so completely, had drained them. They were not invincible. This was my chance. My moment to strike down beings far greater than myself. But what if this was another trick? Another deception?

Why couldn't I see myself winning? No. No, I couldn't do this. I couldn't. They walked toward me, slow and confident. Three of them. A perfect, unified force.

I didn't want this. Why was this happening to me? Why did my own talent, my own strength, warrant punishment? And why a punishment so brutal, so suffocating?

No.

I would not stop.

I would not kneel.

Even if I were to die here, I would make them suffer. I would swing until my arms were torn from their sockets. I would charge until my legs collapsed beneath me. If I had to, I would bite and tear and rip and claw my way through their flesh. I would kill. I would hunt. And then, I let it take me.

The madness.

My vision warped. The fibers beneath their skin became clear to me, and I reached for them. I seized them, plucking their existence apart, thread by thread.

I laughed.

I laughed though I could barely stand.

"Oi, you demonic bitches!" I howled, my voice raw with rage. Another talon carved across my chest, and still, I laughed. "Tell me, do you feel fear?!" Another blow sent me flying, my ribs cracking beneath the impact.

"You will rue the day you decided to enchant me with your petty tricks!" My blade swung wildly, aimless, merciless.

"Aren't you having fun?!"

Because I was. Oh, I was. Blood coated the arena. I no longer knew who was bleeding more. I didn't care. I swung without defense, without hesitation, without thought. And then, I saw it.

Fear.

Their eyes darted to one another. A silent question. How? How was I still standing? I didn't even know the answer. My pride had long since withered. Now, there was only hunger. Hunger for blood. Hunger for the kill.

How marvelous. How beautiful.

The pain was euphoric. The blood is intoxicating. No sensation could compare. And the cherry on top? The absolute delight?

The terror in their eyes. They feared me. A mortal. A nobody. A creature they would have once dismissed without a second glance.

They screamed. I laughed. They had no choice but to fight, but one of them,one of them broke rank.

How delightful.

This was it. The weakness. The flaw.

But I did not strike her down. Not yet. No, I wanted them to witness something far greater. I wanted Athena herself to see what happened when basic strategy was discarded. I wanted her to witness a force that defied norms, that rejected sanity.

I wanted her to witness me.

The moment their heads turned, looking at their sister, my blade struck. Blood blinded them as I forced my weapon toward both their throats.

One head rolled. The second Empousa, the one still standing, caught my blade in her maw. The audacity. I didn't stop. I forced the blade further, through the jaw, skull, spine.

The sound of shattering bone was followed by another sound, one that filled me with loathing. A metallic twang. My blade had snapped.

That corpse. That wretched, worthless corpse. It had broken my sword. I had wielded it for a month. I had grown fond of it. It was mine. And she had the gall to break it. I pounded my broken weapon against her corpse, again and again, until the hilt itself shattered.

No matter. I no longer needed a blade. I turned to the last one, the weakest link, the coward who had tried to run.

I walked slowly, savoring her fear. She deserved it. Her sister had broken my sword. She may not have done the deed herself, but that did not matter. My rage would not be quelled.

I stood before her, waiting.

Would she strike? Would she fight? Would she prove herself worthy of even a sliver of respect?

No.

She sat there, frozen, paralyzed by terror.

How pathetic.

I rained hell down on her. Perhaps I was reminding her of Tartarus. Perhaps I was simply indulging in my fury. She babbled something, some gibberish plea.

I did not care.

I kept swinging.

Five minutes passed. She stopped moving. A bell rang.

But I did not stop.

I struck again. And again. And again. Until her very body faded from existence.

Then, at last, I turned to the notification that had been waiting for me.

Trial Complete.
3 Empousa Slain.

Grade Achieved: A.

Allocating Rewards…
New Skill Unlocked:
Unbroken Swing
A desperate sword strike that refuses to stop, cutting through all in its path as if resistance does not exist. It can only be used when the wielder's body is too broken to swing their blade, driven forward by sheer madness. Though powerful, its force is wild and uncontrollable, leaving the user vulnerable after the strike.

I let my body collapse.

Darkness took me.

And the throne room awaited.

Chapter 27. "The time to relax is when you don't have time for it." , Sydney J. Harris

When I came to, I was in front of the king alone. My body ached, and my mind was slow to piece together where I was, but the sight of him made my blood run cold. I was tense, thinking I was about to be judged once again. I can't handle another trial right now. I need time to breathe, to process, to rest. But much to my surprise, the king's smile was… genuine?

My heart pounded harder. No. No, this wasn't right. This son of Athena had always carried himself like an executioner hiding behind the guise of duty. His anger, his pleasure, his amusement,every flicker of emotion was calculated, a tool wielded with purpose. Yet now, as he stood before me, the face beneath the weight of the crown was one of… contentment.

It unsettled me more than any of his previous cruelty.

"What are you so happy about?" I asked, my voice rough, my throat dry.

"Simple," he said, his voice laced with undeniable satisfaction. "You did what I didn't expect."

I frowned, suspicion gripping me. "Care to elaborate?"

He paused, considering his words carefully. Even now, every sentence from him was deliberate.

"You passed all the trials," he finally said. "And I didn't expect it."

The honesty in his tone was disturbing. He was pleased,no, he was thrilled. That alone put me more on edge than if he had drawn a blade against me. What was his angle? Why was he acting like this was a victory for him?

"You should now be able to view your status. I suppose congratulations are in order," he added, as if I should be honored.

I hesitated, then accessed my status, my heart pounding.

Name: Hudson Mitchell
Rank: Mortal (F)
Class: Light Warrior
Patron #1: Now Available
Patron #2: N/A
Patron #3: N/A

The sight of it made me smile. And then, before I could help myself, I laughed. It was real. My efforts had been acknowledged. The grueling, agonizing trials,I had endured them, and now, I could finally pick a patron. I had no idea how, but I didn't care. This was the first real step toward my own power.

Before I could ask any questions, the doors burst open. My allies returned.

We were together again, and for the first time in a long while, we could breathe.

Their eyes met mine, my body still battered and healing. But instead of hesitation or pity, they smiled. I could hardly believe it. Rebecca and Anna both nodded with an unspoken approval. And Shawn,Shawn tackled me into a crushing bear hug.

"Shawn, calm down, bro, I'm still here, aren't I?" I chuckled, patting his back.

His grip was tight, and for a moment, I let myself accept it. Out of everyone here, I could trust Shawn. He had proven himself over and over, despite his initial doubts about me. A solid ally, one I wanted on my side. I didn't feel the same certainty with Anna yet, and Rebecca was… complicated. But Shawn? He was real.

A sharp cough from the king made Shawn release me. The air shifted as all eyes fell back on the ruler before us. His expression was expectant, like a teacher waiting for his students to settle down.

"I have to admit, the four of you surprised me," he began, sweeping his gaze over us. "I suppose it is time I tell you the truth of why I am here. I was never meant to be your guide."

The weight of his words settled over us. A tension built in the air. He continued before we could question him.

"This was never about guidance. It was a test. A sixth trial, if you will."

Shawn crossed his arms. "Yeah, can you please elaborate on that?" he asked, his tone measured but firm.

The king inclined his head. "Of course. As you all know, my Lady, the great Athena, is the goddess of wisdom and warfare. She does not simply wish to raise warriors, but soldiers of the mind. It is not enough to swing a sword; one must understand the battlefield, the enemy, and most importantly, themselves."

He paced, his steps deliberate. "And so, I tested you. I belittled you. I crushed you. I made you doubt yourself and each other. But I did so with purpose." His voice grew softer, but no less commanding. "Because that is what it means to wield true power."

Rebecca and Shawn exchanged glances. Something about the way he spoke had them considering his words more seriously than I liked. Was he convincing them? Was he trying to shape their minds even now?

I clenched my fists. No, something wasn't right.

"As you can tell," the king continued, gesturing toward us, "you are now ready to choose your first patron. This is a privilege not often given."

There it was again, that subtle pressure, the underlying message hidden in his words.

"Wait," I interrupted, narrowing my eyes. "What do you want from us?"

The king's smile didn't falter. If anything, it grew more knowing, as if he had been waiting for me to ask.

"Why, I don't want anything, Hudson," he said smoothly. "Only to apologise. The hardship I put you through was necessary. And yet, look at you now." His voice was warm, proud even. "Stronger. Sharper. All of you have surpassed expectations. And now, you have the rare opportunity to choose a patron beyond the basic deities of your class."

Something in my chest twisted. How did he know that? How did he know our options when we hadn't even considered them yet?

He wasn't just revealing information,he was guiding us, nudging us along a path he wanted us to take.

"The gods do not reward the weak," he said, his voice steady and unwavering. "They do not grant favor to those who hesitate. The strong survive, and the wise endure. That is why Athena has blessed you with this chance."

Shawn was nodding. Rebecca seemed contemplative. Anna remained silent, watching the king closely.

I exhaled sharply. He was molding us, even now, planting seeds of thought. This wasn't just an explanation. It was propaganda.

"But enough of my words," he finally said, stepping back. "Now it is time. You will meet your new patrons."

With a single clap of his hands, the world shifted. The room dissolved, the air crackling with divine energy. And just like that, we were gone.

Well, at least we were *supposed* to be gone. But only Rebecca and Shawn vanished,Anna and I remained. We exchanged a glance, confirming we had reached the same conclusion. But Anna took it a step further.

"So confirm what we already know," she demanded. It was blunt, bordering on disrespectful, but undeniably effective.

The king regarded us, his expression unreadable. "Anna. Hudson." His gaze swept over us, measured and deliberate. "My lady has an offer for you,one you would be *wise* not to refuse. Both of you have caught her attention with your intelligence and discernment. This is an *honor* the others failed to earn."

Anna and I sighed in unison, likely for the same reason. *Predictable.* But there was no harm in playing along.

"Right," I responded, feigning indignation. "And why should we choose Athena over the deities who have actually watched over us throughout this tutorial?"

The king's lips curled into something between a smirk and a sneer, his voice rich with conviction.

"You see, Hudson, Lady Athena is not just any deity. She is an *Olympian*. A princess of Olympus. Her influence spans realms beyond your understanding. The power she offers is *unmatched*. It would be foolish,*reckless*,to turn down such an opportunity."

But then he slipped up. And he knew it. I could see it in the flicker of realization behind his eyes.

Anna had caught it too. Another glance between us was all it took.

"Do you mind giving us a moment to discuss?" Anna asked smoothly.

The king hesitated, then nodded, vanishing into the ether.

"So, what do you think?" Anna asked, her gaze sharp as she studied me. "It's not a bad offer on the surface." She leaned back slightly, feigning an ease neither of us truly felt.

I let out a short, humorless chuckle. "Anna, let's cut the bullshit. Neither of us would ever consider this crap." My voice was low, steady, but laced with irritation. "Athena is a bitch. A calculating, manipulative bitch who has spent this entire labyrinth ridiculing us, using the king as her tool." I met her eyes. "And that's exactly what she wants from us... She wants us to become tools for her."

227

Anna's lips curled into a slow, amused smile. "Thank the gods you're thinking the same way I am." Her voice held something close to relief, but it was laced with curiosity. "But why do you think she chose us instead of the other two? Wouldn't they be easier to shape into weapons?" She tilted her head slightly, studying me.

I frowned, letting the question settle in my mind. She had a point. The other two,our so-called allies,were more malleable, more desperate for approval. Why bypass the obvious choices and come to us instead?

"I think that's exactly why," I mused, voice growing thoughtful. "They're too easy to mold. Too predictable. She wants a challenge. Maybe for the sport of it, or maybe…" I hesitated, then smirked. "Maybe it's something even simpler. Entertainment."

Anna's smile faded, but the gleam in her eye remained. "Entertainment?" she echoed, testing the word, rolling it over in her mind. "Yes… That would explain the way they watch us, wouldn't it?"

"Their little game," I agreed. "But technically, there's another reason that comes to mind." A grin tugged at the corner of my lips. "And that one fills me with excitement more than anything."

Anna exhaled sharply, not quite a laugh, not quite a sigh. "I was afraid you'd say that." Yet she didn't look dismayed. If anything, she looked...intrigued. "But yes. You're right. There's another, far more likely explanation." She paused, voice lowering slightly. "After all, she isn't just some goddess playing matchmaker between warriors and patrons. She's a princess of Olympus, with responsibilities that go beyond simple meddling."

I caught on immediately, my mind clicking the pieces into place. "She's in charge of eliminating problems before the Thunder Bringer gets involved."

Anna nodded, her gaze sharp. "She doesn't like who's willing to sponsor us."

A silence stretched between us, weighted with understanding. Athena wasn't trying to recruit us out of generosity or even out of some strategic calculation. No, she wanted us out of the way before we could be claimed by someone else, someone who opposed her.

"Exactly," Anna murmured. "Our potential patron must be someone she considers a threat." She let her words hang in the air, waiting, letting me reach the conclusion on my own. A test.

I met her gaze and gave her the answer she was leading me toward. "It could be a Titan." I let the words settle. "Or another Olympian who she simply doesn't like."

Anna's expression didn't change, but I noticed the flicker of something beneath her careful mask, satisfaction. This was more than idle speculation for her. This was a personal calculation, and I was willing to bet she had a strong suspicion about who her own patron was going to be.

"Perhaps," I said, testing my own theory, "our patron is simply someone who goes against her ideals."

Anna's smile was sharp, almost impressed. "Perhaps."

We held each other's gaze for a long moment. A silent agreement passed between us, built on months of reluctant trust, of standing side by side in battle, of knowing that despite our differences, we were cut from the same unyielding cloth.

We turned in unison to the unseen presence listening to our every word.

"We refuse the offer."

For the briefest moment, I thought I heard a scoff; disdainful, unimpressed. And then the world shifted, the air tightening around us as we were whisked away, not by Athena, but by the one who had been waiting for us all along.

Chapter 28. "He who cannot obey himself will be commanded." – Friedrich Nietzsche

Rebecca POV:

It seems as if every deity has an obsession with throne rooms. Grand, gilded, imposing; each one designed to remind visitors of their insignificance. This is the third throne room I've stepped into in just a month. At least this time, it's an opportunity rather than a judgment, or so I tell myself.

What I did not appreciate, however, was the near-blinding radiance of my surroundings. Towering golden pillars loomed on either side, encrusted with crimson gems that shimmered like drops of blood frozen in time. They stretched impossibly high, supporting an azure ceiling so vast and distant that one might mistake it for the open sky itself. The floor beneath me was laid with ivory-white tiles, polished to an unnatural sheen, each one narrowing slightly as they led toward the throne. Towards him.

The sight that met me was both overwhelming and perplexing. A man sat upon a throne, but calling him simply a 'man' felt like a gross understatement. He was taller than any mortal ought to be, his very presence stretching beyond the confines of his body, his existence demanding attention. Around him, animals of all kinds knelt, their heads bowed in reverence, as if worshipping a force far beyond their comprehension.

As I took another step forward, their expectant gazes turned to me. I could feel the weight of unspoken commands, a silent pressure urging me to lower myself as they had. But I would not. I could not. I have never been one to kneel so easily. Let him prove himself to me, not the other way around.

Stopping before the throne, I met his gaze and spoke with measured defiance, my voice unwavering.

"What can you offer me?"

It was the moment I realized my mistake.

The air around him shifted, thickening with an overwhelming, suffocating presence. It bore down on me with such force that my knees buckled, betraying me before I could resist. My breath caught in my throat as the temperature spiked, an unbearable heat searing through my skin until I could feel blisters forming. I wanted to scream, to fight back, but my voice had abandoned me.

Fear.

For the first time in a long while, I felt true fear. And yet, beneath the agony, something else burned; a different kind of heat. An opportunity. A chance for something greater than myself.

Then, he spoke.

His voice resonated through the chamber, carrying the weight of the sun itself.

"My name is **Apollo Sol Invictus**."

At the mere utterance of his name, the throne room trembled. Power rippled through the space, invisible yet undeniable, a force that demanded recognition. His name alone carried a charisma I could not define, an authority I had no choice but to acknowledge.

"While my sister has yet to forgive you," he continued, his golden eyes smoldering with something unreadable, "I think you are still useful."

A chill settled over me despite the lingering heat. This was no mere invitation. It was a declaration. A judgment of a different kind.

And I had no idea what it would cost me.

Shawn's POV:

As expected, I was transported to another throne room. But unlike Erik's, this one was... well, sad. Completely barren. No fancy decorations, no grand tapestries, not even a single torch on the walls. Was this even a throne room? It felt more like a cave someone just decided to rule from one day.

The pillars weren't even proper pillars, they were stalagmites shooting up from the ground, impossibly massive, like nature itself decided to play architect. The floor was nothing but packed earth, and there wasn't even a clear walkway to follow. How was I supposed to make a grand entrance with no dramatic path leading up to the throne? Rude.

The darkness here was different, too. Not the creepy, "something's-gonna-jump-me" kind, but the kind that carried presence. It reminded me of my time on tour, deep in the wilderness, where the night pressed in from all sides, heavy but not hostile. This wasn't something to fear. This was something powerful.

And yet, I stood there like an absolute buffoon.

What was I supposed to do? Say something? Take a step? This was clearly some kind of test, right? Some mind game meant to judge my worth? But I wasn't exactly the brightest when it came to puzzles. If this was an IQ test, I had already failed.

As if the universe itself agreed with my self-assessment, a sudden gust of wind blew from behind me, nudging me forward.

…Oh.

So not a test. Just me being an idiot. Cool, cool.

With my nonexistent dignity barely intact, I took a step in the direction the wind pointed. And then another. But with each step, the air grew heavier, pressing down on me like an invisible weight. It was like carrying a boulder on my shoulders; a boulder that doubled in size with every move.

One foot forward. Another step. My knees screamed. My muscles burned. Oh, this was definitely a workout. Whoever ruled this place better appreciate the effort.

When I could bear it no longer, I finally collapsed onto one knee, thankfully, right in front of the throne. So at least I wasn't completely embarrassing. Small victories.

And there he was.

A goliath of a man sat upon the throne, exuding power in its purest form. He was alone, his presence filling the emptiness like he didn't need anyone else to make this place grand. His posture was regal but effortless, the kind of confidence that didn't need to be loud to be terrifying. His eyes bore into me, but there was no scorn, just something I dared to call pride.

I had no idea who he was. But his sheer strength? That, I recognized immediately. That was something I understood. That was something I needed.

Then he spoke, his voice carrying through the cavern like a force of nature itself.

"Greetings, mortal. I am the **Endurer of the Heavens, Titan Lord, Atlas**."

The weight of the cave seemed to shift, becoming heavier and steadier, like his presence alone held the walls together.

Titan. Wait. Titan?!

Oh. That wasn't great.

I mean, I was pretty sure the Titans were supposed to be the bad guys. That was common knowledge, right? But at the same time… I couldn't deny his power. His absolute, overwhelming strength.

And if I wanted to survive what was coming next, if I wanted to be strong enough, maybe that was exactly what I needed.

Chapter 29. "If you cannot see where you are going, ask someone who has been there before.", J. Loren Norris.

As I regained consciousness, the first thing I noticed was the blood. It coated the floor, splattered across the walls, and hung in the air like a suffocating mist. The sight was grotesque, yet there was an undeniable beauty to it, a twisted reminder of both victory and pain. The trophies that lined the hall, broken and fallen, still gleamed with a faint, defiant lustre, their former grandeur stubbornly clinging to their shattered forms.

The mouths of these trophies seemed to turn towards me, as if alive, as if they were made for me. But they were stained, covered in the blood of those who had once sought them. I could feel their silent judgment, their expectations, but I refused to acknowledge them. The magic, the divinity, the meaning they once held was irrelevant now. They were merely symbols of a past I no longer cared to remember. I moved on, walking past the remnants of what was once glorious, my steps heavy with defiance. At the end of the hall, a red carpet stretched out before me, untouched by the chaos I had left behind. So I walked until a different sight before me

The next room was lined with weapons, each one laid out with meticulous precision. But unlike the trophies, these were untouched by blood. No, they gleamed; sharp, polished, and perfect, their edges reflecting the dim light with an unsettling clarity. Once again, they seemed to point toward me, their posture as audacious as the trophies before them. It was almost comical. These weapons, the very tools of violence, were pristine, devoid of any carnage they were meant to inflict. They should have been soaked in blood, heavy with the scent of death, yet they remained pure, immaculate.

And yet, in that strange contrast, it dawned on me, the weapons, not the trophies, were the true symbols of power here. The trophies had been broken, their luster dulled by time and ruin, but these weapons; they were made to last, to cut, to conquer. They were the silent, unyielding rulers of this place. It was a sick joke, the things that should be stained with blood were not, while those meant to be kept pristine were tarnished beyond recognition. But I cared not for the symbolism. It was irrelevant to me now. I had already passed through the halls of victory and defeat, and whatever the meaning behind this place, I had no interest in finding it.

At last, I reached the end of the room, only to be confronted by yet another door. This one, unlike the others, did not open on its own accord, but it felt inevitable, as if it had been waiting for me all along. I pushed it open, and there, in the center of the next chamber, sat a throne. It was grand, imposing, and somehow familiar, as if it had been waiting for the one who would come to claim it. The weight of the room shifted, and I knew without question: whatever this place was, whatever trials I had endured, it had all led to this moment. The throne awaited, but who sits upon it?

I walked slowly toward the throne. Each step echoed in the vast, hollow chamber like the beat of a war drum. The air grew heavier the closer I came, thick with a presence that clung to my skin and gnawed at my mind. And then I saw it; his silhouette, seated, still, watching.

And then I *felt* it.

An aura unlike anything I'd ever known. It was unnatural. Suffocating.

A primal instinct surged through me; bloodlust, pure and unfiltered. My hands itched to draw a blade, to tear, to maim, to bathe in destruction. It wasn't fear that gripped me. It was a *need*.

But the moment our eyes locked, it shattered. I couldn't move. I couldn't breathe. I couldn't act. I knew that if I made one wrong move, if I dared draw my weapon, I would be dead before I even understood how.

Yet amid that terror, something else stirred. A purpose. A path. A finality. I wanted to surpass him.

Not defeating him in combat, that was a child's dream. I wanted to rise beyond him, to eclipse him. To become something greater than even *he* had become.

But I saw him. And I understood. He wasn't a man. He wasn't a king. He wasn't even a god in the stories I was told.

He *was* war.

Not the avatar of Ares, the savage and reckless. Not Mars, the disciplined strategist of the empire. No, this being was something older than myth, deeper than symbol. He was war in its rawest, most unfiltered truth. Pure. Ancient. Elemental.

He looked at me not with disdain, nor amusement, but with recognition.

He saw himself in me. A younger, more volatile echo. He knew what I was,what I could become. The same hunger ran through us, the same call to arms, the same dance with death.

But he had *mastered* it. He had bent it to his will.

His path wasn't forged by conquest alone, but by *dominion*,over blood, over fear, over the very nature of conflict. He had not just fought wars. He had become the *law* of war itself.

I did not kneel.

I felt the expectation in the air, thick as iron. A command, unspoken yet absolute. But I stood tall. Unmoving.

And I saw it,the faintest flicker of approval in his gaze.

Still, I had to speak. I had to acknowledge what stood before me.

I opened my mouth, voice steady but reverent.

"I greet the God of War."

Silence. That was his answer. A silence so deep, it pressed against my skull like a vice. But I knew. I *knew*. It wasn't indifference , no, he was still *watching*, dissecting me with eyes that had seen a thousand empires burn.

Then, after what felt like a century trapped in stillness, he spoke.

"It is good," he said, voice like steel scraping against stone, **"that you did not call me what I am not."**
He stepped forward, each movement bending the air as though the world itself yielded to his weight.

"I am Ares."
He said it with the 's' silent; a pronunciation ancient, older than the Greek, older than *language* itself.
"I am War incarnate."

The words weren't just spoken. They *arrived*; carried on the backs of armies long dead, echoing with every scream ever lost on a battlefield.

"I come from an age before memory. My younger forms whispered of you. They say you are more *me* than *man*. There is war in your marrow, not the chaos of mortals, but the *purity* of it. A rare thing."

He stopped. Waiting. Testing.

I bowed my head, not in submission but in strategy.
"Thank you for your grace," I said carefully. "What must I do to earn your tutelage?"

A sound broke from him, a low, contemptuous laugh,
like a blade being drawn across bone.

"You think you are here to earn *me*?"
The air thickened as a sliver of his aura bled forth.
Oppressive, ancient, commanding. For a moment, I felt
the battlefield stir beneath my feet, though none existed.

"Insolent. But amusing."
He withdrew the pressure, and I could breathe again.

**"It is irrelevant. I have already *chosen* you. There is
no test. You accept… or you *perish*."**

His presence was not one that followed a script. He *was*
the script. The universe didn't move around him; it
moved *because* of him.

I inhaled, steady. Calculating. "Then I thank you for your
benevolence. May I ask… what rewards follow such
divine selection?"

He tilted his head, not angered. Intrigued.
"Greedy. Ambitious. Arrogant."
A pause. Then a smile, sharp and cold.

"Good."

**"It is that defiance I enjoy. You are still unshaped…
Wild, undirected. But there is potential. And I… shall
indulge it."**
He raised a hand.

"Consider this... your first taste."

Blessed Skill – Chthonic Wrath (Phase I: Ember of War)

Type: Passive/Active Hybrid | Unique to Ares' Champion

Description:
The blessing of Ares stirs from dormancy, kindled by the violence it craves. Every blow struck by the Champion is not merely an act of war, it is a prayer, an offering that feeds the ember burning deep within the soul. This ember grows with each wound inflicted, awakening the first echo of the ancient chthonic force sealed beneath the god's crimson mantle.

Lore Note:
"War is not a skill. It is hunger. The Champion does not learn to fight… He remembers."

I felt it, pure, undiluted power surging through me like wildfire in dry veins. My very blood pulsed with it. The skill, it wasn't just active, it was *alive*, woven into the fabric of my being. For once, my trials had been answered, the silence that mocked me now shattered by divine revelation.

I turned to the towering figure before me, no mere man, but a god. His presence wasn't just felt, it was crushed. Oppressive, ancient, unrelenting. The weight of war incarnate. And still, I met his gaze and offered my thanks.

"Thank you for your gift."

I knew this wasn't the whole of it. He'd said as much himself. A taste, a fraction. I wasn't special, I was *useful*. Chosen not out of need, but for potential utility. One day, I'd serve a purpose. And he'd be watching.

"Be honored, mortal. This is no petty boon," Ares intoned, his voice like grinding stone. He didn't wait for me to reply, he wasn't here to converse. He was here to declare.

"You've felt it, haven't you? The pull of violence. The taste for destruction. You were always aligned with war, but this world you've stumbled into, it's deeper than you can yet grasp. You are far too fragile for the full truth. So I offer you the barest bones, and even that is a mercy."

He leaned back, sprawling into his seat like a lion at rest, though not at peace. That was my cue.

"Understood. Please... tell me more." I tried not to sound desperate. I wasn't begging. I refused to. But I was *listening*.

He chuckled. It shook the air.

"Your impertinence is amusing."

Then his tone shifted, iron replacing ash.

"Then let me speak of truths few mortals have ever heard… Truths etched into the marrow of the cosmos. Among the divine, there are four pantheons whose dominions shape fate and time. The Greco-Roman, mine, is the oldest and greatest. The Norse,storm-born and prophetic. The Celtic,wild, eldritch, steeped in primal rites. And the Egyptian,silent monarchs of death and return.

We are not stories. We are the hands behind history, the architects of catastrophe and salvation alike. Where empires rise, we watch. Where kings fall, we laugh.

And you, *you*, were chosen.

At first, it was curiosity. A flicker. But beneath your flesh, we saw potential. A fracture in the mundane. I, Ares, Firstborn of Olympus, God of War, Warlord of Immortal Legions, Slayer of Titans, and He Who Commands the Red Storm, was the first to mark you. Not out of grace. Out of ambition.

Your power is unbridled. Truly unstoppable as it is wild. But raw power is the tantrum of beasts. You will not be a beast.

You will learn. War is not merely blood and blade. It is pattern, strategy, symphony. You shall study the anatomy of annihilation, the geometry of conflict, the laws of divine supremacy.

And now, your weapon."

His voice grew darker, heavier.

"This is no tool of steel. It is a relic forged in the crucibles of forgotten stars, quenched in the ichor of slain deities. It is bound to you, not to serve, but to challenge. It is your test."

Xyphos of the Chthonic Ares.

And then, *it* spoke.

"Oh. You're the one he picked? Hah. Of all the screaming mortals clawing for scraps, he chose the little feral thing, breath like blood, eyes like war. How charming.

I was forged in a moment of divine boredom, shaped by hands older than Olympus, deeper than any shrine. Not out of love. Not out of need. But because he wondered what would happen if he gave a spark to a storm waiting to be born.

I am not your teacher. I am not your friend. I am not impressed.

Swing me with purpose, and I *may* awaken. Slaughter with meaning, and I *might* grow. But flail like a fool, and I'll stay exactly as I am, silent, sharp, and disappointed.

Now go on, little chaos thing. Show me why he laughed."

Arrogant little blade. It thought it owned me. We'd see. I would tame it. Or it would tame me.

Then, Ares stood, not with ceremony, but with the finality of a closing gate.

"You will be enrolled. Tomorrow, you will awaken at the Academy. Where mortals shed their skins and prepare to ascend. There, you will learn to identify gods, earn relics, and walk the path of power. If fortune favors you, perhaps you'll inherit a battle art, or forge your own.

But that is for tomorrow."

"Wait, what is it that you mean?" I asked, hoping to gain some sort of insight into what is to come. He waited for a moment then he raised his hand, and the world grew dim.

"*...you are dismissed.*"

And just like that, I was alone.

I found it a bit rude that he would do such a thing. But regardless, it seems I need to go to university again to progress. With nothing left to do, I opened my status screen.

Name: Hudson Mitchell
Rank: Stirring Initiate (E)
Class: Light Warrior (new available)
Patron #1: Ares (Chthonic Olympian: greco-roman)
Patron #2: N/A
Patron #3: N/A

This was it, the power I had been waiting for. The sensation was unmistakable, like a storm gathering quietly behind my ribs. A stirring initiate… that is what I am. Not yet a blaze, but a spark trembling with potential. A flame on the cusp of awakening. And I can still evolve, that is the truth I hold above all else.

Then something shifted. I felt it in my hand, the card. It pulsed faintly, as if responding to my resolve. A message shimmered into view. It seems the time has come… I can choose my next class.

With steady breath and a touch of anticipation, I reached out and placed my fingers on the symbol etched into the card. The moment my skin met the surface, it came alive, glowing with ethereal light. Slowly, it unfolded before me, revealing a list of paths, each a promise, each a challenge. My future lay in the space between them, waiting for me to decide.

Gravecutter

"He moves like someone who's already dead. Only the sword lives now."
Gravecut is calm in a way that unsettles. He's cold, direct, and silent in combat. That is until he strikes.

Then, it's a sudden flicker of steel, a burst of precision, and back to stillness. The madness is buried deep. But it's there. Watching.

Well, thankfully it keeps the sword. But to be honest… that's about it. I don't really know what this class brings to the table. It feels empty. Maybe it would be worth something if we got actual skills with the class — but that's not the way this world works, is it? We take what we're given. Still, I kept reading, hoping for something. And sure, there was a pretty quote to dress it up, something poetic to make it sound enticing. But it just felt off. Not wrong, just… not me. This class is made for someone who waits. Someone who sits in silence, plans things out, waits for the 'perfect' moment. Patience, restraint, timing, that's not who I am. I see that as a coward's victory. A step back before you strike? Why would I do that? I don't step back. I don't wait. I move forward. I break through. That's who I am. That's all I've ever been. Oh well, maybe the next one is better.

Splitjaw

"His sword moves one way. His body moves another." A Splitjaw's style is jagged, wrong, and unpredictable. He bends and contorts mid-fight, turning what should be openings into traps. His sword doesn't follow form, it's all feint, whip, twist, and ambush. There's something broken in how he moves.

Hmm, not bad. Definitely an improvement from before. Even the pretty quote feels sharper, more fitting. What grabs me most about this one is the unpredictability, there's a certain chaotic beauty in it. It feels… right, somehow. Like it actually reflects the madness I carry. But even with that, one question keeps burning in my mind: how the hell is this class supposed to change my battle style? Didn't Ares say something about learning a battle art? Were these classes meant to be hints, or just foundations? Because right now, it's not clicking for me. It just doesn't make sense.

And to be completely honest with myself, I'm pretty sure I lack the flexibility or finesse to make this class truly thrive. It requires a kind of fluidity I don't think I have. And while that's frustrating, I have to accept my own limits. I have to be realistic. So I pray that the last one, whatever it is, is the one that fits me best. The one that finally feels like mine.

Ironhowl Swordsman

"He doesn't parry. He doesn't wait. He answers pain with more of it."
The Ironhowl is a swordsman who channels his madness into momentum. Every blow he takes feeds the rhythm of his attacks, a relentless chain of wild, snapping swings. The howl isn't for fear. It's to drown everything else out.

Okay it seems like fate is on my side. Or should I say the fates? Oh well it doesn't matter. The point is this is a class which near perfectly describes my style. But nevertheless the burning question remains. What in the actual hell am I meant to do to progress? I needed answers. What does this mean in combat? Does this change my mindset or what? I don't even get skills, isn't this far less rewarding than the tutorial itself? I am genuinely confused. Then I look down at what I'm holding in my offhand, an ego sword.

"Hey, any advice?" i asked

"Did you not understand my initial speech?" it exclaimed

"Relax yourself swordy, i just want some answers"

"You called me fucking swordy!" it shouted

"Well you didn't give me a name, also what happened to your noble demeanour?"

"My lord is not here i don't really care anymore, also my name is Aelysk Mor'Krath"

"Right, that name is very easy to pronounce", I responded while rolling my eyes, "can i call you alex?"

"No"

"Mr A?"

"No"

"Mr Mor"

"I AM A WOMAN"

"Didnt know swords have gender."

"Well now you do"

"Okay how about Krath?"

"Acceptable"

"Okay then can you please give me any sort of advice?"

She paused for a moment before finally caving, "I suppose I should at least do the bare minimum, your class signifies the first step onto your battle art, you will actually learn to make your battle art in the academy. The knowledge and basic style and necessary strength will be ingrained in you, however don't choose something that doesn't feel right. Trust the thing that our lord chose you for. Your instinct."

After thanking Krath I instantly chose it, the class that called to me, the class that I didn't need to renew myself for, I chose the Ironhowl Swordsman.

Chapter 30. "The trust of the innocent is the liar's most useful tool." , Stephen King

Anna POV:

It was strange, how ironic it is that I had to leave Earth to finally feel free. To escape the chains of my old life, I had to cast myself into a world far more dangerous than anything I had ever known. Constant threats of death lingered in the shadows, and the risk of imprisonment hung over every choice I made like a blade. Yet somehow, despite it all, I felt liberated. Strangely, wonderfully liberated.

Most of the people I travelled with were decent, good, even. The only one who might be considered 'bad' was someone who reminded me too much of myself. And now I see the truth that eluded me for so long. The reason I felt so trapped... it was never the world. It was her, my sister. The one I dedicated everything to. The one I thought I had to protect. She saw me as her delicate little sister, someone soft and breakable, someone who needed her strength to stand.

But I don't.

It's not bitterness that pushes me now. Not resentment. I don't rise to spite her or to prove something shallow. No, my wings unfurl for something deeper, something purer. Freedom. Freedom is power. And I have no intention of surrendering that again.

Coming to this world was just a taste, a fleeting glimpse of what lies ahead. And I won't squander it. I won't be a pawn like Shawn, obedient and blindly loyal. Nor will I fall into the trap of reckless defiance, as Rebecca did. I saw what power looked like during the tutorial. It was cathartic. For the first time, my suffering wasn't for nothing. It was the prelude to something greater. I know I'm not alone in that. Others must have felt the same, a caged soul hiding behind a mask. A woman, silenced by her own false image. I maintained a persona that clashed with every thread of my being, and I'm done with that. I will no longer bow to a life of quiet endurance. I will rise to thrive.

As I walked through the corridor, I ignored the grandeur around me. The towering pillars seemed to loom like silent sentinels, but I did not meet their gaze. I knew instinctively: to be distracted was to fail. Not a test from some deity waiting at the end, but a test of my own making. A test of my resolve. My conviction. I must be unshakable. I must never lower my head to one who has not earned it. That is who I am now.

Beneath my feet, the ground changed. Dust gave way to polished marble. The ruins behind me slowly transformed into opulence, until I found myself inside what could only be described as a palace. The corridor became a corridor no longer, it was a procession. A path toward something ancient, something sacred.

My thoughts drifted back to the tutorial. The lies I spun with effortless grace. No one suspected a thing, except *him* of course. I cloaked myself in innocence, in those wide, trusting eyes my sister always adored. She was right, in a way. My eyes *are* beautiful. But they have always concealed far more than they revealed.

Back then, I used the only strength I had to survive. But now? Now I walk with purpose. I will use my strength to rule. To reshape. To *reign*. Perhaps that is why the deity chose me. Not for my morality, but for my potential.

The throne came into view, and with it, a weight settled on my shoulders. Familiar. Oppressive. Ancient. The onyx throne stood tall, its surface gleaming like still water at midnight. It was not empty of meaning. Every etching, every symbol, whispered of trials long passed. And at its center, a sigil confirmed what I had begun to suspect.

He was my patron.

The youngest of her children, who defied destiny and carved his own path. The one who ruled through both awe and terror. Beloved and feared. A deity whose ambition nearly brought the end of his own pantheon. The crooked one. The First King. The one who wielded a divine weapon forged by the Earth Mother herself. The true king of the Greco-Roman line.

And his throne was empty.

I paused, expecting him to materialize, to greet me, test me, claim me. But time dragged on, and silence stretched too long. My patience, already thin, snapped.

My greed won.

I stepped forward. Left foot first. Each step up the dais felt sacred. The engravings along the stone brushed against my fingers like cold fire. And then, without hesitation, I seated myself. My legs rested. My posture straightened.

The throne was no longer empty.

And at that moment, *he* appeared.

Not beside me. No. His throne dwarfed mine. Towered above it. A masterpiece of cosmic craftsmanship that made mine look modest by comparison. He didn't speak. He didn't need to.

I looked him in the eye.

And without a flicker of fear, I spoke:

"I greet the King of Titans. The Crooked One."

Epilogue

In a room veiled in shadow, a chamber where stone bled memory and the air held the scent of rust and rain, sat a man. He was alone, yet not alone, for the room knew him. It was memorable.

The figure sat in silence, draped in a form not worn in ages, smiling with a grim satisfaction. The chains at his feet did not rattle, they pulsed, like veins filled with molten iron. He had chosen his first champion. One. Just one. That was all he ever needed.

Too many others, too many thrones, too many *lesser* gods, had spread their favor thin. Mortals tripping over divine gifts they neither earned nor understood. He had watched it for centuries, no, *eons*, and finally, he had acted.

Then came light. Not sunlight. Not warmth. Light like an idea taking form, golden and beautiful and uninvited. Apollo entered the chamber. And the light recoiled from the walls.

"Brother," said the god of prophecy and radiance, "Father would not be pleased that you've taken this shape again."

The man who sat, *the Ares beneath the surface, Ares of the earth's iron heartbeat*, lifted his head slowly. His eyes were dull red, like coals gone cold, yet still burning somewhere deeper.

He gave a breathless, joyless laugh. "Must I remind you, Apollo? *Your* father is *your* king. He is not mine."

Apollo's gaze, ever-seeing, narrowed. "He rules two-thirds of you. That still binds you to him, whether you whisper it or howl it."

"I am not Mars or Ares," Ares replied, his voice like iron grating on stone. "Mars was forged for the empire. Ares thrived in the drama. I was born of slaughter. I have never found a worthy champion. Until now."

Apollo's mouth tightened. "I see what you're doing. You cloak it in righteousness, but it is ambition. A plot."

But before further accusation could rise, the atmosphere shifted. Grace entered, not gentle, not soft, but graceful like a blade honed by centuries.

She entered not like a guest, but like a queen inspecting her own war camp. Her beauty was a weapon. Her step, a drumbeat.

"Greetings, Lady Astarte," Apollo said, bowing with rare sincerity.

Ares did not rise.

"You greet her with respect," he said. "But not me?"

"She did not belong to our court once. She chose to become *Aphrodite Areia*. She chose us, and in this form, she deserves true reverence."

Astarte's eyes, dark and knowing, lingered on the two brothers. Her voice was velvet steel. "Don't think I don't see through the fire and light. Both of you dance around your intentions like cowards."

"Do not chastise him," Ares said, finally rising. When he stood, the floor did not tremble, but the shadows deepened. "The chains he bears were gifted by *our* king. As were mine. And neither of us asked for them."

"Hush, beloved," Astarte said, placing a hand over his. "Even my husband stirs. And you know, he is my first loyalty. The tools he forges now… they hum with dread. That alone is enough to concern me."

"There is no concern in me," Ares said. "Only preparation. Let the old man fret over omens. I bend to no fear, and no throne. I bow to one king only,*our* king."

And then the world answered.

No door opened. No figure stepped forth. The sea itself seemed to arrive. The floor grew slick with unseen moisture. The walls wept salt. And the air thickened, pressure, like the crushing dark at the bottom of all oceans, settled on their bones.

A voice filled the room. Not spoken. *Known.*

"I trust you have chosen your champions well."

It was not thunder. It was not breathing. It was deep, the kind of sound that makes the spine remember its earliest fears.

The three younger gods fell to their knees, not in ceremony, but instinct. As prey freezes when the true predator enters.

This was no Olympian ruler, no skybound tyrant. This was the slayer of the Titan King. The bearer of ancient law. The one who gave away half his power not out of virtue, but because it was too vast to wield alone. The one who walks between sea and soil, dream and grave.

He was *the king beneath the storm*.

He had no need for names. His presence *was* a name.

"This cycle's trial," the voice continued, "was granted to the pantheons. A whim, born of my queen's unrest. And yet, the ancient law endures. I may not have a champion for myself. So I watch. And I judge. Do not disappoint me."

There was no roar. No flash. Only silence, and the fading echo of something that had *never truly left*.

The roman vanished first dragged not by force, but by knowledge. Some chthonic truth had touched him. And it had been too much.

Then the king was gone.

Not a trace remained, yet the air did not ease.

Ares remained standing, though he leaned slightly toward Astarte. And she stood firm, eyes searching for something no longer present.

They said nothing for a time. But both knew.

This was no longer about mortals. Not truly. This was about gods. Their place. Their reckoning.

And beneath their feet, far beneath,deeper than Olympus, deeper than Hades, something stirred.

Printed in Dunstable, United Kingdom